"Quit gathering wool and scrub these plates. I've got to use them to serve that new table of folks."

Esther swiped her arm across her forehead, smearing the sweat around. "I don't know why everyone decided tonight was the night to grace us with their presence. I've only got one shepherd's pie left. Hope it's enough. I've never run out of food." She threw plates on a tray and hurried back toward the dining room.

Lainie glared at the sink full of suds and dishes. Her hands would never be soft again after all the time she spent with her hands dunked in the burning water. Mama would be horrified, but Mama couldn't stop her. And Lainie had come to like her little room. She wouldn't leave until she had a job here and had made her way. If that meant washing dishes by the sink load, she'd do it. She dove into the pile of dishes with a sudsy rag.

She hummed a hymn as she worked. "It is well with my soul." The words filled her mind with peace and replaced the tightness around her heart. She continued to hum and pondered the words.

Could it be well with her soul when everything around her had fallen apart? Her dream of serving in Europe lay in ashes around her feet. Her health still hadn't recovered, though she had more good days now. She didn't have the job she needed. . . yet. But peace flooded her heart.

She longed for a way to bottle the feeling, to seal it in her heart for those moments when the fear and disappointment overwhelmed her. Elbow-deep in the water, she sang the words until they saturated her heart: "It is well with my soul. It is well, it is well with my soul."

CARA C. PUTMAN lives in Indiana with her husband and three children. She's an attorney and a ministry leader and teacher at her church. She has loved reading and writing from a young age and now realizes it was all training for writing books. An honors graduate of the University of Nebraska and George Mason University School of Law, Cara loves bringing history to life. She is a regular guest blogger at Generation NeXt Parenting and Writer Interrupted, as well as writing at her blog, The Law, Books & Life. Check out her Web site at www.caraputman.com. If you enjoy this book, be sure to read *Canteen Dreams* and Cara's upcoming *Captive Dreams*, which will release later in 2008.

Books by Cara C. Putman

HEARTSONG PRESENTS
HP771—Canteen Dreams

Sandhill
Dreams

Cara C. Putman

Heartsong Presents

No book is a solo endeavor. Thanks so much to my first readers, Sabrina Butcher, Sue Lyzenga, and Janna Ryan, and to Tricia Goyer for sharing her time and experience. Thanks also to Emilie Eros and Virgene Putman for investing in my children while I raced toward a deadline. And last but certainly not least, many thanks to Tom Buecker, curator of the Fort Robinson Museum, who freely gave of his time, knowledge, and extensive files during my visit. You made the war at the fort come alive. Tom's book, *Fort Robinson and the American Century*, is fantastic.

And special thanks to my editor, JoAnne Simmons, who believed in this series of World War II stories. It has been an honor and a privilege to work with you.

To Eric, for always believing I would be more than a one-book wonder and for cheering me from those first words. . ."So did she tell you she wants to be a writer?" Looking forward to seeing what the next fifty years hold!

A note from the Author:
I love to hear from my readers! You may correspond with me by writing:

Cara C. Putman
Author Relations
PO Box 721
Uhrichsville, OH 44683

ISBN 978-1-60260-010-2

SANDHILL DREAMS

Our mission is to publish and distribute inspirational products offering exceptional value and biblical encouragement to the masses.

PRINTED IN THE U.S.A.

one

As a child, Lainie Gardner had known that the rocking of the train, the clunk of the wheels on the tracks promised adventure, excitement, but not this time. Sitting on a train headed to the farthest corner of Nebraska was the last thing she had imagined for her life. Her dreams shimmered in the distance like a mirage. She should be crossing the Atlantic Ocean with her friends and fellow nurses from the Ninety-fifth Evacuation Company, bound for the European front. Instead, she waited for the train to stop long enough for her to disembark in Crawford.

She tugged a lace-trimmed handkerchief from her jacket pocket and wiped a small circle on the train window. Dust blew in waves across the desert landscape of the Sandhills. The few trees squatted against the horizon. The emptiness mocked her, mirroring the barrenness inside.

The conductor swayed between the seats of the car to the rhythm of the clacking wheels. "Next stop, Crawford." Even his words were as lifeless as the tumbleweed that paced the train.

The train jerked from side to side as it slowed. People jumped from their seats and collected their items. A dark-haired toddler jostled against his mother. He jumped on the seat, and his sandaled foot slipped. Lainie sucked in a breath. With a thud, his head collided with the hard bench seat, and he wailed. He raised his head, and Lainie noticed a gash on his forehead and a trickle of blood.

Lainie attempted to jump from her seat to help him but stopped short. Her joints refused to unlock. Not too long ago, she'd been active and healthy, but not anymore. Rheumatic fever had struck quickly and left her weakened and vulnerable.

The commanding officer's words raced through her mind. *"Young lady, being a nurse requires strength and stamina, of which you have neither."* Oh, she'd fought that pronouncement, but in the end, she lost.

The boy's mother pressed a handkerchief against the wound. Lainie sighed and collapsed back on her seat. There was little more she could do to help this young boy. But she could have done much for the soldiers.

"Next stop, Crawford." The conductor continued his travels through the car.

Lainie shuddered and then swiped the cloth across her forehead. Her stomach knotted, and doubts raced. She'd skipped the planning that would make this trip a success. "I must be crazy."

The matron across the row quirked an eyebrow as she glanced at Lainie.

Lainie blushed. The words weren't supposed to trip from her mouth like the tumbleweeds blowing across the hills. She fingered the veil of her hat and turned back toward the window, ignoring the questions reflected in the woman's eyes. She'd answered too many questions already. No need to entertain a stranger's.

The click of the train's wheels against the track slowed its tempo. She tucked her paperback book and handkerchief inside her handbag. The knots tightened their hold as she wondered what she'd find at Fort Robinson, a few miles down US Highway 20 from Crawford.

Crawford would seem like a hamlet compared to North Platte. She shuddered. North Platte had never seemed like much of a town to her. Not that it mattered now. She couldn't go back to what her life had consisted of before she left for nurse's training. A cycle of endless parties and flirtation held no appeal after she had tasted the opportunity to make a difference.

Lainie pitched forward when the train jerked to a stop. She leaned down to look out the window, and her heart sank as she fell back into her seat. "There isn't much to Crawford."

"No. It's a small extension of the fort and a few ranches. But those of us who call it home love it." The matron's steady voice soothed the fear that gripped Lainie. The woman searched Lainie's eyes a moment before she continued. "This your first time here?"

"Yes, ma'am. I'm hoping to get a job. You know, free a man to fight and all that."

The woman pursed her thin lips, a pinched expression settling on her sharp features almost as if she'd heard that story many times and watched others' hopes crumble. "Yes. Well, good luck." The woman's ample form sidestepped into the aisle, freeing Lainie to stand.

Lainie almost ducked to look under her seat for her courage. It had been in full force when she had convinced her family that moving to Fort Robinson was the right step. With the girls from the Ninety-fifth Evacuation Unit shipped out, she'd thrown caution to the wind, packed her bag, and bought a train ticket in the opposite direction and a few thousand miles closer to home.

She sidled down the aisle toward the door, a tightness and deep ache pulsing from her muscles. She swallowed against the pain. The effects of rheumatic fever lingered, and the train ride had been harder than she'd anticipated.

Loud, almost frantic barks ricocheted off the train as she stepped onto the platform. She shielded her eyes and scanned the area. She stepped toward the wooden crates stacked two high and at least six wide. Snouts and paws pushed against the chicken-wire fronts. The barking escalated as two men placed an additional crate on the pile.

The dungarees and cowboy boots they wore with their khaki, standard-issue shirts made her wonder if they were soldiers. Yet this uniform was a far cry from those the servicemen wore as they rushed through the canteen back in North Platte. One slipped back into the car while the other wiped his forehead.

"What is all this?" She raised her voice over the din.

The soldier reached into the gaping maw in the train's side to accept one end of another crate.

Lainie pulled herself to her full height, all five feet and a couple of inches of it, and leaned toward him. "Excuse me."

The soldier dropped the crate he'd picked up and spun on his heel, rubbing his ear. His gaze took her in then swept over her again. "You didn't need to shout."

Lainie thought she'd never seen eyes as clear blue as his, without a hint of iciness. He ran a finger over a scar on his hand, almost like a forgotten habit.

"Had to make sure you heard over the barking."

The soldier closed his eyes and rubbed a hand over his face. She couldn't tell if he was frustrated with her or trying to hide a smile. "Ma'am, you've made me drop valuable Department of War resources. If that animal's injured, my officer will have my hide."

"Why don't you check and see?"

He leaned down, careful to keep his face a good three feet from the wire. "It's a quiet one. I hope that means it's fine. If you'll excuse me, I have a job to do."

His words ricocheted through her mind. Yes, he might have a job, but how could unloading dogs in Nowhere, western Nebraska, be important to the war effort? He didn't have to rub her nose in it.

Balling her fingers into fists, she stomped toward her suitcase. The dogs' continued barks pierced her head and made her long for a quiet room. She scanned the platform, and her heart sank as she realized no one remained who could help her. She plopped on top of her suitcase, shoulders slumped.

Well, there was one man who could help, but she wasn't about to ask.

❧

Thomas Hamilton chomped down on his lower lip as he tried to ignore the dogs stacked around him and the young woman stalking away. He'd almost told her she had a swipe of soot across her forehead, but then the crate had dropped. The mark added a hint of frailty to her appearance, but he figured she'd be horrified to know it existed, even if it didn't mar her dark beauty one bit.

"How many more?" he mumbled to his partner. "The conductor looks anxious to move on."

"Just a minute." John Tyler disappeared into the dusk of the car. A skinny string bean of a man, he fit easily inside the cramped area. Tom had tried it once and decided he'd rather be trapped in an underground cave for hours than be surrounded on all sides by nervous dogs in a space with little to no room to turn around. John's feet stomped against the wood floor. "It looks like we've got six more crates. How are we supposed to get all these mutts back to the fort?"

Tom eyed the crates and shrugged. "We'll fit on as many as we can. Worst case, I make two trips. You wait here with what won't fit."

"No, you cool your heels while I drive back and forth." John crossed his arms and stared at Tom.

Tom held his position. It wasn't his fault the army had decided he could best serve by working with dogs. Dogs of all things. Who in their right mind joined the military and expected to spend day after day surrounded by yipping, yapping, barking, four-legged nuisances? Certainly not him. No, he'd come here to work with the herd of horses. And with thousands at the fort, that had seemed like a safe assumption. But this was the army, and plans changed. So John could stare all he wanted. Tom would not babysit crated dogs. Maybe he'd get orders to ship out soon. Others had and now saw action in Africa or the Far East. A guy could hope.

"Fine." John took off his work gloves and threw them on the ground. He jumped off and walked toward the stack of crates. "Let's get the last crates out of here."

With a grin, Tom slapped John on the back. "Now there's a reasonable plan." In no time, they'd stacked the last crates on the platform. "I'll back up the truck. Don't worry. It won't take long. In no time, I'll collect you and the last dogs."

John grumbled under his breath as he followed Tom.

They worked quickly, loading the crates and tying them down in record time. All the while, Tom watched the young spitfire pace the platform before sinking onto her suitcase. Now that she'd left him alone, she looked lost and uncertain. As if she hadn't a clue what to do next.

Her fingers twisted the handle of her bag as her gaze flitted around the platform. She glanced at him, and her back straightened. He smiled as he watched her force her shoulders back and tilt her chin. She was a petite thing, not even hitting his shoulders, and her dark hair and porcelain skin reminded him of movie stars like Elizabeth Taylor and Linda Darnell. The beauty had spunk. He'd give her that. Even if she looked out of place on the wooden platform. Surely she'd gotten off at the wrong place, misunderstood the conductor. She looked as if she was better suited to a city like Denver than to the wide-open expanse around Crawford.

"Are you done lollygagging and ready to finish this job?" John eyed him with the hint of a smile tipping his lips. "I think I'll spend the time I'm waiting to ask that nice-looking dame to Mrs. Babcock's for pie. Sounds like a good way to spend the time."

"And what would Naomi say about that?" John's cute wife had a steel backbone anytime John stepped out of line.

John rolled his eyes and did a jig along the platform. "She'd say I made a good addition to the welcome committee. Let's get you off to the fort."

Tom glanced back at the woman and noticed her watching them. He stilled as she stepped toward him, picking up speed as she walked.

"Excuse me. Did I hear you say you're headed to the fort?"

Tom nodded until he could find his voice. "Yes, ma'am. I'll leave in a minute."

"Wonderful. Could I catch a ride with you? It's important I reach the fort today."

Tom turned to block John's glare. "Ma'am, do you have an appointment or other reason to travel to Robinson? I can't give everybody who wants space a ride. One of the shuttles can take you later."

She chewed on her lower lip and glanced away. "I don't have an appointment. Surely that doesn't matter if you have a space."

John harrumphed behind him. Tom rubbed the back of his neck and considered his options. There wasn't a clear rule, but civilians didn't get rides. "I'm sorry."

"Fine." Fire flashed from her eyes. She squared her shoulders and turned on her heel. He watched her stride across the platform. She turned back. "If you won't help, at least point me in the right direction."

"Don't tell me you intend to walk."

"You've left me no other option." She looked from him to John. "Maybe you'll be so kind as to point me toward this shuttle."

John rubbed his hands together. "How about a slice of Mrs. Babcock's pie first?"

"You're as impossible as he is. I'll find someone who'll help." She grabbed her suitcase and stalked toward the small station. If she was lucky, she might find someone in there. Likely Ed had closed up and headed for lunch now that the train had moved on. She rattled the door and drooped when she couldn't get in.

"For crying out loud." He couldn't leave her there like that. Tom hopped in the cab of the truck. "John, I'll be back soon as I can."

He eased the truck to a stop next to her. She remained focused on the road in front of her. "Hop in." He jumped out and opened the passenger side door for the woman. "Please. My mama raised me better than to let you walk."

A pallor had settled on her face, highlighting bright spots on her cheeks. "Are you okay?"

She stopped. "I will be." She turned to him, and a thin

smile graced her lips. "Thank you." She accepted his hand and climbed onto the seat.

"John, come grab her suitcase, okay?" Tom settled behind the wheel of the truck and looked at the woman. "We'll get your suitcase later; the back's too full right now to squeeze it in. Where do you need to be dropped off?"

She glanced at him then back out the windshield as the truck pulled away from the station. "I'm not really sure. I'm here to apply for a job, so the administration building, I guess."

Tom scratched his head and swerved to miss a wheel-sized hole in the road. The roads weren't used to all the traffic the war had brought to this small fort tucked in northwestern Nebraska. One he'd never heard of before enlisting a year ago. "By the way, I'm Specialist Thomas Hamilton. All my friends call me Tom."

"Lainie Gardner. I appreciate the ride." She eased against the seat and closed her eyes.

Concern flooded him. "Are you sure you know what you're doing?"

Her eyes flew open. "Of course I do. Why would you think different?"

"Well, you don't seem to have a plan, Miss Gardner. Don't you think it would have been a good idea to have a job before making the trip?"

"Certainly not." Her lips firmed into a hard line.

two

Lainie fumed and stared straight ahead, expecting the man's laughter at her plight. If she weren't so angry, she'd laugh herself. She'd done it this time. She was stranded in the middle of nowhere, without a job or a place to sleep. Now she bounced around the cab of a military truck with a strange soldier. Her mother would be horrified.

Tall outcroppings of white rock pushed through the Sandhills to the north of the highway. Their ragged edges revealed how centuries of rain had molded and shaped them. The formations were unlike anything she'd seen.

"What do you think of the buttes?"

"Is that what you call them? Lovely." She turned and stared at the man. "That it? Your best attempt at conversation? Asking what I think of the scenery?"

"Other than continuing to mention you're a fool to come without a plan? I thought the view was safer."

Lainie snorted. "You don't understand women, do you?"

Color crept up his neck in a way that would have been endearing if she weren't so annoyed. "Women overrun the fort. Wait until you see the hordes."

"All the more reason for me to come."

"Sure. And in two weeks, you'll be married and unwilling to work."

"You are insufferable." She jostled against the door, her backside connecting with the firm bench. "Ouch." She resisted the urge to rub the ache away.

The landscape flattened as they barreled down the road. A row of buttes pushed up the earth at an angle from US Highway 20, which laced the plain. Prairie grasses grew with trees scattered along the ridges, but the majority of the landscape was wide open. Barren. Like her heart. Shattered like her dreams of joining the war effort. Lainie clenched her teeth and vowed she would talk her way into a job at the fort.

"Look. I'm sorry we got off on the wrong foot." The soldier whipped his cap off with one hand and rubbed his forehead. "You have every right to be here. So why did you come? You don't seem like the type to run up here without the semblance of a reason."

"Thanks, I think." Lainie smoothed her skirt, and her fingers played with the navy worsted wool fabric, twisting and untwisting it. She eyed him. Was his apology honest? She sucked in a breath and decided to treat it as such. "My mom read an article in the *North Platte Bulletin* about the push for civilians to free enlisted men to ship overseas. I can help."

"Why not stay in North Platte or wherever you're from?"

"I had other plans that didn't work out. And this is far enough away from home to keep my folks from hovering."

"What can you do?"

"I'm trained as a nurse but need something less strenuous. I'll take clerical work." South of the highway, row after row of narrow wooden buildings lined a road. It looked like a hastily constructed camp or barracks. "Is that part of the fort?"

"That? No, it's a prisoner-of-war camp. Construction's pretty much done, and the first prisoners should arrive in June or July."

Lainie hadn't expected to see such evidence of the war this close to home. Soldiers—at least she assumed they were soldiers in their jeans—walked between the buildings, but none looked at the truck. What were they doing if they didn't have prisoners to guard? She pushed a piece of hair behind her ear as she turned her attention back toward the highway.

"How long have you been stationed here?"

Specialist Hamilton shrugged. "Since I enlisted. I thought I could help with the horses and signed up here twelve months ago. However, the army, in its wisdom, decided I'd work with war dogs. So here I am, a private specialist who works with canines all day." His fingers tapped against the large steering wheel. "I'm hoping to ship overseas soon."

"Where's home, soldier? You don't sound like a native Nebraskan." Lainie smiled as the routine questions she'd used at the North Platte Canteen flowed.

"A little bit of here and there, but mostly Wyoming." The truck crested a slight hill. "Here we are."

Lainie gaped at the fort spread before her, filling both sides of the road with activity.

"That bus coming toward us is what you'll take to get to the fort in the morning. It shuttles folks back and forth from Crawford."

"Okay. So what should I expect to see?"

"Scattered around here is a herd of around four thousand horses in various stages of enlisting and mustering out of the army, and a herd of mules mustering in and training. The British Army appreciates our well-trained mules." He looked at her and quirked an eyebrow.

A pleasant shiver chased down her spine, and she smiled. "Where are the dogs housed?"

"Off that way. We train them at the War Dog Training Center to the south of the highway. There's plenty to keep us busy out here."

She pulled her attention back to his words and wrinkled her nose as she tried to decipher them. "War dogs?"

"Dogs. Mutts. Heinz 57s. Whatever you want to call my cargo. They get shipped here from all over the country courtesy of Dogs for Defense."

"What do you do with them?"

"We train most as sentries. A few get shipped back to their owners if they don't have what it takes. The others proceed to advanced training." He turned right into the compound and stopped the truck in front of a two-story brick building. "Here you go. The private inside can direct you to whoever you need to see."

Lainie stared at the building. Every certainty she'd had that this was the right step washed from her as she considered what she had to do next. She urged her limbs to cooperate, to propel her out of the truck and up the stairs, but she couldn't move. As she sat there, Private Hamilton bounded from the truck and opened her door.

"Look. My mama always told me to treat a lady well. A lady waits for her door to be opened." He swiped his hat off his head, wiped his forehead, and offered a slight bow. "It's been a pleasure."

She looked into his kind eyes and saw the friendship he offered. "Thank you for the ride, soldier." She accepted his proffered arm and climbed out of the truck. Jutting her chin out, she gripped her bag and walked up the wooden steps to the building.

She hesitated a moment then pushed open the door. Stale air thick with cigarette smoke threatened to choke her. A thin man behind a metal desk nailed her with a glare. "Can I help you, miss?" Derision dripped from each word.

Had any of these soldiers received training on how to welcome people to base? It sure didn't seem that way. By the stripes on this one's shoulder, he wasn't the person she needed to talk to. "I'd like to speak with the commanding officer, please. I'm here for a job."

"Do you have an appointment?" The man looked at her as though he knew she didn't.

Lainie stood straighter and looked down at him. "No. However, he'll want to see me anyway."

"Miss, I don't know where you came from, but you don't belong here. We are not a temporary agency, nor do we invite random citizens to park themselves here. I suggest you move yourself out of this building and off this base. We do not have time to entertain young ladies."

With each word he spoke, heat slipped up her cheeks. She clenched her fists and tensed. Lainie knew she should hold her tongue, take whatever he had to say, and hold her ground. But before she could stop herself, she erupted. "Excuse me, but you have no idea what's brought me here. I have volunteered with the North Platte Canteen, serving soldiers like yourself when their trains stopped for a quick break. I received nurse's training and enlisted with the Army Nurses Corp. My unit is currently headed overseas."

"But you aren't with them, are you?" He sneered. "I would think that if you aren't good enough for them, you certainly wouldn't be for us."

"I am here because I can no longer serve as a nurse. However, I can still free a man to serve, and you have civilian openings. I would like to speak to your commanding officer." *Even if a job means I have to work with an arrogant man like you.* She forced a tight smile on her face.

"If you hurry, you might catch the next shuttle to Crawford. If you're really lucky, you might get to town in time to catch the final train." The impossible man had crossed his arms and leaned away from her. He couldn't appear less interested if he tried.

The fight left Lainie. She'd deluded herself into thinking she could accomplish something here. Without another word she turned and left the building, letting the screen door slam. She looked around the parade grounds for the shuttle and finally found it as it headed toward Crawford. She slumped against the outside wall. Maybe Daddy had been right. She should go back to North Platte and give up any thought of doing something important. She could dance the war away at the canteen while she waited for the troubled times to end and her life to begin again.

Where are You, God? Haven't You taken enough from me? She closed her eyes, relieved to feel the pressure ease.

A plan formed in the shadows of her mind.

She'd walk to town, but not to catch a train. She pushed her exhaustion to the side and trudged down the stairs. Surely someone had a room she could rent. One foot in front of another, Lainie reached the highway. Her breath came in gasps as shards of pain pulsed in her joints. She looked back and groaned. The administration building was only a couple of blocks behind her.

So there wasn't a job waiting for her. There had to be a way. And if there was, she was the woman to find it. If only she could make it back to Crawford.

three

The din from almost fourteen hundred dogs pounded Tom's ears. Row after row of waist-high wooden boxes stretched across the field. He grimaced and pulled his hat lower to muffle the noise. The cacophony echoed day and night across the compound past the barracks, almost back to Crawford. Some days, he'd give a month's salary for ten minutes of quiet.

He pulled in front of the War Dog Reception and Training Center. It sat low and squat against the horizon, looking as if it had grown out of the earth from its concrete foundation. Inside that building, the dogs he transported would get a cursory inspection and be released to the quarantined kennels to recover from their journey. Then they'd be inspected, weighed, groomed, and inoculated and remain in quarantine for a week. Then these animals would receive a trainer, start basic, and run through their paces until they understood key commands.

Several men ran up to the truck as soon as he popped it out of gear.

"What did you bring us today, Hamilton?" Sergeant Lewis strutted to the truck and slapped the top with his beefy hand.

Tom jumped at the noise and opened the door into Sarge's stomach. "Just the routine load of German shepherds, collies, and a Great Dane or two. I think I saw a Lab, as well."

"Watch it." Sarge backed away and grimaced as he rubbed his stomach where the door had connected. "Someday they'll quit sending us hunting dogs that chase every scent they pick up."

"It'll take a bigwig or two on sentry duty with a Lab who gets a whiff of some animal. By the time the dogs drag them back to base, they'll listen."

"Let's get these off-loaded." Sarge looked around. "Where's Private Tyler?"

"Waiting with several we couldn't fit on."

"What kind of pie does Mrs. Babcock have today?" Sarge smacked his lips.

"She was getting off the train, so I doubt she whipped any up yet."

"That woman's amazing. I bet she had one in the oven the moment she arrived."

Tom smiled at the thought. She enjoyed taking care of the soldiers. Did more than her part to keep morale high as far as he was concerned. Soldiers often fought to slip into Crawford and wander by her boardinghouse. Inevitably, they left with their stomachs stuffed with thick slices of pie and a glass of fresh, creamy milk.

The woman and her pie worked wonders on lonely soldiers.

Several men hustled about and emptied the truck of its wooden crates. Others hauled the crates inside where soldiers would release the dogs. Days like this, Tom was particularly glad he wasn't a vet tech. Little sounded worse than examining a bunch of scared dogs minutes after they'd arrived. A sure recipe for attacks. Maybe if he slowed down the trip back to Crawford, he could avoid processing, too. Then all that would be left when he returned would be introducing a couple of the dogs to the wide-open prairie. That he could handle.

Private Donahue yanked on the last crate, and Tom hurried to help him ease it to the ground.

"I'll go get the rest." Tom climbed back into the cab.

"Hurry back, Private. We need to talk about your dogs."

Tom stifled a groan as his stomach clenched. He wiped the sweat drenching his palms onto his pant legs. "I'll rush back, sir."

"Be sure you do. Would hate to have to send a team out to find you." Sarge stalked into the building behind the last dog team.

"Sure thing," Tom snapped.

Several soldiers snickered, and Tom rolled his eyes. They didn't understand his fear a dog would attack him or his hope that with each set of dogs that shipped out with its new handlers he'd get reassigned. Foolish, but he hoped nonetheless. Anything to get a change in assignment. Dad had promised his fear would disappear at some point. Tom doubted it, especially after a year of close encounters with his four-legged friends. He snorted. Dogs might be man's best friends, but they'd never been his. Still mumbling, he turned the vehicle around and headed out.

He hit the open stretch of highway between the fort and town, and his thoughts turned back to the spitfire to whom he'd given a ride. There was something captivating about her—even if she had been all sparks. He slowed when he saw someone on the side of the road. The woman stumbled along, holding her shoes in her hand. If it weren't still early afternoon, he'd wonder if she'd been drinking as she staggered around with stiff motions. He pulled to the side and slammed on the brakes. That gal, Miss Gardner, didn't even turn.

"Lainie? Miss Gardner?" Tom ran the few steps to her side. She turned glazed eyes on him. "Can I give you a ride to town?"

Fatigue pulled her features down, even as her gaze darted about as if looking for options. He settled back. If she thought she had a better way, fine. But he was her only option, whether she wanted to believe it or not, and he wanted to help her.

Finally, she looked at him and smiled. "I don't want to be a bother."

"The bus won't be back for a couple of hours. It's not out of my way to drop you off."

Color flashed up her cheeks. "Thank you. You seem to be the only one with time to help. And then my heel broke."

"It might be your air." He shrugged his shoulders to soften the words.

"My air?"

"Well, we're not used to people acting like they own the place."

"I don't." She sputtered to a stop. "Okay, so maybe I have. I tend to do that when I'm unsure. I don't belong here any more than I do on some battlefield."

"Then let me help. Hop in." He offered her his arm. She looked at him, hesitated, and then accepted it. With her light touch on his arm, he felt a shock wave of electricity shoot straight to his heart. *Steady, boy.* It hadn't been that long since a beautiful woman had accepted his help. There was something different about this woman, though. When he searched her eyes, he saw a woman whose dreams had been replaced with emptiness. It made him want to overlook the ways she lashed out, because like one of the injured dogs he helped, the growl meant she was hurt.

"Anything I can help you with other than the ride?"

"Know of a job for me?" The corner of her lips quivered.

"Wish I did. You'd think they'd be searching people out. It's a bit isolated for some."

"I can see that. The sky stretches forever here. Do you like it?"

"I grew up in Wyoming and followed my father from ranch to ranch. He was a vet and got called at all hours to help with sick or injured livestock. That part of the country isn't much more populated than this." Tom paused and looked around, trying to see the place through the eyes of a newcomer. "It may seem desolate, but I see God's creativity. He could have settled on fertile valleys or the ocean as the perfect landscape. Instead, He created this area between the Rockies and the farmland to remind us of His bigness. It might be rough, but it's got an innate beauty. You just have to look for it."

Lainie's lips curved upward. "I do believe you have the soul of a poet hidden underneath that uniform. The land has captured you."

"I hope its Creator has, ma'am."

"Maybe it's the heart of a preacher buried in your soul."

Tom wrenched away from her searching gaze. That was the first time anyone had called him a preacher, and he couldn't quite label how that made him feel. Was he too transparent with a stranger? Or too reserved around his friends? He chuckled wryly.

Rubbing his forehead, he slowed the truck. "I don't know about that. But I do know something about this place grabs me. Now where can I take you?"

"I don't know. I'll need my suitcase, but I have no idea where to stay tonight."

Tom smiled. This was an easy problem to fix. "Mrs. Babcock's it is."

"Mrs. Babcock?"

"She has a restaurant and a small boardinghouse for young women. If she doesn't have room, she'll know who does."

Lainie pulled in a shuddering breath. "Okay."

He stopped the truck in front of the station. Hopping out, he said, "Wait while I get your bag."

Tom looked up to see John Tyler watching him, arms crossed over his chest.

"About time you got here. What's she doing with you?"

"Things didn't go as hoped. I'm running her to Mrs. Babcock's and will be right back."

John slouched against the stack of crates. Metal clanged, and loud barks filled the air.

"Thanks for waking them up, Tom."

Tom shook his head and walked back to the truck. "See you in a few."

"Yeah, yeah."

It took approximately two minutes to cross Crawford and pull the truck near the white picket fence that surrounded Mrs. Babcock's three-story Victorian. The house looked oddly oversized to Tom each time he pulled up. He supposed for her line of work, running a boardinghouse with a small restaurant on the first floor, it was perfect.

The sun's rays reflected off the fresh coat of paint that a

group of soldiers had applied three weeks before. Clumps of plants struggled to grab a foothold in the rocky soil around the front porch. Even a load of manure hadn't helped.

"Here it is." Tom turned the ignition off and tapped the wheel with his hands.

Silence greeted him. He looked at Lainie, saw her swallow. She looked near tears. He fought panic. What would he do if she broke down and cried?

She swallowed again. "There isn't much to Crawford, is there?"

"You should have seen it before the war. And the people are friendly. I think you'll like it here. If things don't work out, I'm sure you can always go back to wherever you came from."

She turned from him and swiped at her eyes. "You're right. It will be great. I'll feel better when I know I have a place to stay."

"Mrs. Babcock has a heart of gold. You'll see." As Tom helped the young woman up the stairs, he prayed he was right, because suddenly he didn't want to see Lainie leave.

four

May 15, 1943

The sun's warm rays tickled Lainie's cheek. She peeked at the light and groaned. She hadn't slipped into a nightmare. She truly lay in a strange bed, in a strange room, in a strange town.

The room felt tiny, with barely enough room for the narrow bed, an oak vanity, and a heavy wardrobe. Floral wallpaper decorated the walls, and a rag rug covered the floor next to the bed. Its rose and blue colors brightened the room. She only wished her spirit was as bright.

She curled up in a ball and pulled the quilt over her head. She should have listened to everyone who told her to stay home.

No. When she'd boarded the train to Kentucky, determined to make a difference for whichever soldiers she nursed, she'd set her course. To go back would prove to everyone she was still a child in need of care.

She pinched her eyes shut and scrunched her nose. Maybe if she wished hard enough, the world would miraculously right itself. The war would end. The boys would return home. And she would regain a life of ease. Was that what she wanted? Did it fit her anymore?

Someone stomped down the wood floors of the hallway. Lainie pulled the covers down and opened her eyes. A knock shook the door in its frame.

"Still in bed, Lainie? Get up or you'll miss breakfast." Mrs. Babcock's alto voice filtered through the door. The woman had welcomed her last night and led her to this room as if she'd long expected Lainie to occupy it.

Lainie tried to relax from her tight ball, but her joints fought her. The train ride and her ill-fated walk had pushed her weary body too far. Pain seared her arms and legs. She gritted her teeth and breathed deeply. One. Two. Three. She exhaled and relaxed her muscles.

"You okay?"

Lainie grimaced. "I'm fine. I'll be down in a minute."

"All right." The words sounded doubtful, as if Mrs. Babcock expected her to turn over and ignore the day.

Lainie sat and pushed off the bed. After a moment, her limbs unlocked, and she staggered to the wardrobe. She opened the door and stared at the clothes. The day stretched in front of her with nothing to fill it. She didn't have anyone to impress. She reached for a serviceable navy skirt and white blouse then stilled when she spotted her red sweetheart blouse. The town would surely flood with soldiers for the weekend. Yes, red was perfect.

Moments later, she tugged a brush through her curly hair and straightened her skirt. She slipped down the stairs and headed to the dining room. Dirty dishes loaded one table. A few scrambled eggs and a slice of toast were all that remained at the buffet.

Mrs. Babcock bustled through a door, a stained apron tied tightly around her ample middle, arms filled with plates of bacon and pancakes. "Here's some fresh food, missy. Please make it down with everyone else in the future. Breakfast is at seven o'clock sharp."

Lainie's mouth watered at the crisp aroma of bacon. "Yes, ma'am. Smells wonderful."

A smile tipped the corner of Mrs. Babcock's mouth. "I serve nothing but the best here. This particular slab of bacon came from Elmer Jackson. He does something that makes it extra smoky. Enjoy."

"Since I'm the only one here, why don't you join me? I can help clean later."

"It would feel good to sit a bit. It's been a long morning."

Lainie glanced at the clock on the buffet. She hated to think how early Mrs. Babcock had gotten up if she thought 8:00 a.m. constituted a long morning. After Mrs. Babcock shoveled three pancakes and four slices of bacon on her plate, she bowed her head. Lainie stared.

"Don't mind me. I hate to miss an opportunity to tell my Lord thank you."

Lainie nodded then stabbed a piece of pancake and ran it through the maple syrup pooled on her plate. She savored the sweet bite and dove in for more.

"What are your plans for the day?" Mrs. Babcock dabbed her lips with a napkin.

"I need to find a job at the fort. The gentleman I spoke with yesterday was less than encouraging. Apparently he hadn't heard the fort needs civilian workers."

Mrs. Babcock scooped applesauce on top of her pancakes and smeared it around. "Availability of jobs depends on who you know. What do you want?"

"To be on a boat crossing the Atlantic. But I'll settle for anything."

"You've got ideas. Otherwise, you'd be at Kearney's Air Base working a factory job or a base in Lincoln or Omaha. Folks don't come to Robinson without a specific reason."

Lainie studied her plate. She didn't know this woman or whether she could trust her with her hidden hope. Mrs. Babcock waited.

"I've never done anything that mattered before. Somehow I have to contribute to the war. My best friend, Audrey, works at the North Platte Canteen."

"I've heard of it. Boys rave about it. Did you volunteer?"

"From the first day. But I have to do more than give cookies and fruit to soldiers. I planned to nurse." Lainie swallowed against the pain. "But that died when I got sick. I have all the training but can't use it. I guess I'm typing pool–bound."

"So you type?"

"Never tried, but I can learn."

Mrs. Babcock smiled and pushed back from the table. "I know what we'll do after the dishes, then."

Before Lainie knew what had happened, she found herself standing beside Mrs. Babcock in the kitchen, drying dishes. After what felt like hours, the last teaspoon and glass were tucked into their spots in the cupboards and drawers.

"Follow me." Mrs. Babcock bounced down the hallway, quite a feat considering her girth. Lainie giggled as she followed behind. "I have the ticket to get you ready for the typing pool." Mrs. Babcock pushed open a door with her hip and waved Lainie in.

"Welcome to my office. You'll care about the typewriter sitting on that small table over there. You'll type fifty words a minute in no time."

Three hours later, Lainie decided her idea of practice and Mrs. Babcock's didn't match. At all. Everything from her fingers to her shoulders and back ached from sitting huddled over the typewriter for so long. And her ears hurt from Mrs. Babcock's constant instructions. *No, not that finger. Raise your wrists. Feet flat on the floor.* She was worse than a drill instructor in the army. Lainie had proven to be all thumbs as she fumbled to copy a newspaper article. She'd had no idea typing had rules.

When Lainie had decided she couldn't take one more minute, Mrs. Babcock stood. She grabbed her hat from the desk. "Enough of that."

Amen. Lainie stood from her chair then stretched her arms to work out the kinks.

"Now we head downtown for lunch, and I'll introduce you to folks who can help."

"Maybe the typing pool isn't a good idea."

"Nonsense. You'll get better; give yourself some time."

Lainie groaned at the thought. Kindhearted as Mrs. Babcock was, she had no idea what kind of project Lainie could be. "Did I mention I dropped typing in high school?"

"No, but you have enough training to be inefficient. And

quit calling me Mrs. Babcock. You've got me looking over my shoulder for my spinster aunt, God bless her soul. *Esther* will do just fine, especially seeing as you're a boarder."

Lainie smiled. She'd accept any offer of friendship. She followed Esther down the hall and watched as the woman pinned a floppy hat to her bun. Esther certainly had her own sense of style. "I'll grab my handbag and be right back." Lainie hiked up the steps and slipped into her room. She grabbed a navy pillbox hat from the wardrobe and pinned it to her upsweep. She swept red lipstick across her lips and then studied her reflection. Yes, she would make the right kind of impression. A confident woman who knew what she wanted. She straightened her skirt and eased down the stairs.

After walking a block past small houses dotting Third Street, Lainie followed her hostess to Second. Silence hung between them until Lainie wondered what had happened to her order-barking hostess. They strolled up Second toward what Lainie assumed was Main Street. With each block, the houses thinned out, replaced by businesses. In the business district, the buildings were constructed of brick or wood, and none of them stood taller than two stories.

Cars and trucks lined the streets in front of the storefronts. The ranchers had hit town for supplies. Lainie looked around and noticed that something was absent from the scene. "Where are the soldiers?"

Mrs. Babcock sniffed and crinkled her nose as if she'd caught a whiff of a boarder's soiled laundry. "Look here, missy, if you want to find a beau, you'd better get back on the next train south and return to your canteen."

Lainie stopped and stared at her. "Excuse me?"

"Look at you. All dressed in red with red lips to boot. You are a walking advertisement for a date."

"There is nothing wrong with wanting to look one's best."

"Honey, this ain't no excursion. If that's what you're looking for, maybe you need to head up to Rapid City and gawk at

Mount Rushmore. If you stay around here, the only thing folks'll gawk at is you."

"While I would like to see Mount Rushmore, I highly doubt I'll draw the same attention. Of all the suggestions. I am no floozy."

"I doubt we'll see many soldiers down here today. Those with Class A passes usually seek greener pastures in other towns." A sly sparkle danced in Esther's eyes. "Instead, I want to introduce you to some of the ladies in the civilian pool. If they like you, you're halfway to a job."

Lainie's shoulders slumped. This was not what she'd anticipated when they had left the boardinghouse. All that hiking and pretending she felt fine, but no job. "Lead on."

They strolled into Mae's Diner. Red-checked oilcloth covered the tables, and a mason jar stuffed with silverware and napkins graced each one. Four women huddled around a center table, talking with gestures flying. It was a wonder no one got slapped. Esther waved Lainie forward. "These are some of the gals who work over at Robinson. Barbara Scott is in the post headquarters along with Naomi Tyler." Lainie nodded at the two. "Mary Nelson works with the war dogs, and Liz Czaplewski floats."

In minutes, Lainie hovered over a slice of apple pie and a cup of steaming coffee. The women rushed over each other's stories about working at the fort. Lainie's mind spun with the mass of information. Not even the coffee could keep her mind focused on the forest of details.

It was a relief when the redhead, Naomi, jumped up.

"Sorry, gals, but I've got to scoot. John'll be looking for me."

Liz sighed. "Ah, the life of newlyweds."

"That's right, sister. Can't keep him lonely at home." Naomi grabbed her hat and bag then wiggled her fingers in a salute. "Until next week."

One by one, the girls finished their drinks and slipped away. Esther and Lainie followed Liz out then walked home. Once she returned to her room, Lainie pulled out her hat pins and plopped the hat on her vanity. She eased onto the bed and relaxed against the pillows. After a full day, she'd come no closer to a job. What should she do?

The next morning, Lainie walked the couple of blocks to the First Christian Church she'd noticed during Saturday's excursion. She entered the wooden chapel and found a spot on a bench several rows from the door. Families and an occasional soldier sat in the pews. Lainie sat waiting. . .for something. Instead, she felt nothing. Emptiness dogged her steps. Ever since she'd gotten sick, it seemed God had turned His back on her. She'd prayed to no avail. He surely knew her dreams of becoming a nurse, yet here she sat in a strange place, in the body of a ninety-year-old woman. Crawford might be a new town, but she was dealing with the same God. One who didn't seem interested in her anymore.

five

The German shepherd pulled hard against the lead, and Tom hung on. He would not allow this animal to best him. Warrior: The name fit the beast.

Tom hated working Sundays but had to get this dog and others like it introduced to the prairie. Tomorrow a fresh unit of men arrived, eager to dive into their training. So after the chapel service, that thought propelled Tom across the prairie with this dog.

A handful of dogs needed an assessment before being assigned. Tom and the cadre stationed permanently at the fort had to guess which dogs were suited to which man as quickly as possible after fresh men and dogs arrived. The process went smoother if he walked the dogs around. If only the dogs didn't sense his reservations so readily.

Warrior took off to the right, chasing the shadow of a prairie-dog scent, no doubt. Tom yanked hard on the lead. The dog didn't break stride, and Tom found himself flying down the hill toward the obstacle course. Crazy dog would get them hurt if he didn't slow down.

"Need help, Hamilton?"

Tom couldn't stop to locate Sid Chance's voice. His ankle twisted in a dip, and he grunted around the rush of pain. Warrior collapsed on his haunches, and Tom flew by him, finally flopping down in a tangle of lead, dog, and feet.

"We'll change your name to Brer Rabbit. Sure you aren't part Lab?" Tom glared at Warrior, who grinned at him, tongue hanging. "So you like a good run to start your day. I'll make a note of that." Tom whipped off his cap and ran a hand across his sweaty forehead. He shook his head and then slapped the cap back in place. "You'll be a handful for your trainer. Show me some of that intelligence shepherds are famous for." He'd assign Warrior to a military policeman and see how the two weeks of basic training went. If Warrior survived that, there'd be advanced training for six to ten weeks. If Tom had to guess, Warrior was headed to sentry duty.

Footsteps sounded behind Tom, and he turned to see Sid and a dalmatian headed his way.

"Haven't painted her yet?"

"No. Sarge decided to wait until right before the dalmatians ship out to paint them. I guess that'll signal they're really in the army." Sid plopped beside him. He rubbed his hands along the dog's sides in a relaxed manner Tom envied. "Ready to train the new group?"

"Sure. Then they get to handle the dogs."

Sid rolled his eyes and flopped against the dog, using her like a pillow. "You've got to relax, Tom."

"Don't you think I know that? Some things run too deep."

"Where's your faith in God when you really need it?"

Tom grimaced at the challenge. He wanted the guys around him to see God was a real, vibrant force in his life. He couldn't change that he'd been afraid of dogs since one attacked him as a kid. If working with dogs nonstop for a year hadn't cured his fear, Tom didn't know what could. "I know God could take care of this fear, but He hasn't chosen to."

"Have you asked Him?"

Tom rubbed his neck. Sid wasn't letting him off easy. To be fair, Tom couldn't think of the last time he'd asked God to remove his fear. He knew what to expect from fear. Dogs, on the other hand, were unpredictable beasts. But then a parade of the friendly ones he'd worked with marched through his mind. He shrugged away the image. "Didn't you have a Class A pass this weekend?"

Sid looked across the obstacle course to the highway and buttes beyond. "Yeah, but my girl told me she's not mine anymore, so I stayed here. No sense wasting a good weekend moping."

Silence fell between them. After a bit, Tom struggled to his feet. "Time to get these dogs back to their homes."

"Yep. Only another twenty to check."

Tom hiked up the hill, Warrior walking at his side as sedate as a newborn calf. "Now heel, you fraud."

❧

Monday morning, Lainie eased down to breakfast bright and early, ready for a cup of coffee. Today she'd find a job at the fort if for no other reason than necessity. Esther hadn't heard of anyone in town who needed help, but Lainie would make those rounds, too. Gingerly she touched her fingertips together. She could feel each hour she'd spent Saturday and Sunday pounding the typewriter. She hoped a typing test wasn't required. She still missed more letters than she nailed but had developed more speed in her inaccuracy. Maybe they'd take her word that she was a quick learner.

"Hurry or you'll miss the bus." Mrs. Babcock's words grated in the early morning quiet. Tanya Johnson, the remaining boarder at the table, shoveled food into her mouth even though she didn't take the bus. A quiet gal, she worked downtown at the library rather than at the fort. The job suited her bookish looks and personality.

Lainie shoved the last bite in her mouth. "I'll see you tonight, ladies."

She'd have to fly to make it to the pick-up before the shuttle left. Today felt like a good day. She didn't ache intensely and could move with relative freedom. Maybe the reminders of the fever would lift with time. The doctors in Kentucky had warned her of the possibility she'd feel the effects for life, but this morning her body ignored that prognosis.

The bus driver eased to a halt when he saw her. "Need a lift, ma'am?"

"Yes, sir. Can you take me to the post headquarters?"

"That's a stop. Hop on board."

Lainie settled against an empty seat and prayed today would be different from her last attempt. Hope chased her steps. She smiled and enjoyed the sensation.

One hour later, Lainie struggled to remember the hope she'd sensed. The same surly private refused to give her access to anyone who could help her.

"Go home, miss. There's nothing for you here. If you're set on working, go somewhere else. The Women's Auxiliary Corp is here, and that's all the single women this outpost needs." He turned as if to dismiss her.

Lainie bristled at his condescending tone and treatment. Sure, there might not be a job here—though she doubted that. He should, however, treat her with the common decency all people deserved. She stood rooted to the floor and stared at him. She'd wait to get his attention.

Color crept up his neck, but he focused on the report in front of him.

"I'm a quick study. I know how to type and am practicing to get faster. I can file. I have nursing skills."

"Then join the Red Cross. Look, we don't need you."

Lainie sputtered. The door behind the private's desk opened, and a man stepped out. His uniform bore sharp creases and the silver leaves of a lieutenant colonel. His nose was sharp, but wrinkles softened his eyes, perhaps indicating he enjoyed a good laugh. This had to be the post commander.

"What's the issue, Jamison?"

"This woman insists she needs a job. Here. Hasn't followed procedure."

The colonel turned toward her. "Ma'am?"

"He won't even give me an application. I traveled here Friday because I heard you needed civilians to free men for other jobs. I'm here, and I want a chance."

The colonel examined her, and heat climbed her cheeks. He gave a slight nod. "Private, make sure you take her name and information. Ma'am, I don't know that we have the right posting at this time. However, if you can make the effort to come here, we can take time to explore options. Good day."

"Thank you, sir." Lainie watched the colonel leave. Then she turned to Private Jamison. "Looks like we need to talk." She wore her sweetest smile and leaned against his desk. "What would you like to know?"

Her momentary sense of victory evaporated as the insufferable man sent her out without a job or even a typing test. She left the building and stood on its broad porch, an uncomfortable repeat of Friday. She was stranded on base for two hours waiting for the shuttle.

Lainie eased down the steps and followed the road to the right. Officers' quarters and barracks ringed that side of the parade grounds in front of the headquarters. Brick buildings stood next to simple whitewashed wood structures. Soldiers hurried past her along the road and sidewalk. Most tipped their hats as they rushed past, but none stopped to talk. If only she had something to rush to. She'd rarely felt this useless and alone. The flow of soldiers eased. Lainie smiled as some soldiers eagerly stopped. In no time she felt like Scarlett O'Hara at a picnic, surrounded by a crush of admiring men.

When the bus lumbered to a stop in front of headquarters, Lainie was sorry to see it. Twenty minutes later she sat at the kitchen table, peeling potatoes for supper and spilling her woes to Mrs. Babcock.

"I can stay here for a few days without a job, but not much longer before Daddy'll have to send money." Her face twisted at the thought. She could imagine his response to the request. Something along the lines of "Come on home where I can take care of you."

Lainie squared her shoulders and set her chin. She'd stand on her own two feet. But without a job. . .

"I could use some help around here. Several items on my spring cleaning list haven't been checked off yet." Esther looked up from the pies she was crimping. "The gal who usually helps decided to marry a GI. Doesn't need this job anymore. I'll give you room and board in exchange for your help."

"And a dollar a day on the days I work more than a morning."

Esther smiled. "All right, then. We have a deal."

The days passed, and Lainie believed Esther had received the better end of the bargain. Lainie's hands had never been so chapped from dishwater. And her body ached from the physical activity followed by an hour or two practicing her typing. Each afternoon after she'd finished the day's tasks, she'd change and head downtown.

She walked from storefront to bank to restaurant. No matter how often she asked or how big she smiled, each owner denied needing help. With each no, she wondered if she'd ever hear a yes. There had to be more than cleaning rooms and washing dishes.

If there wasn't, she didn't know how much longer she'd last.

One afternoon when she couldn't take another no, she slipped out to the fort. She considered going to the administration building but couldn't muster the energy to deal with the arrogant private.

Instead, she turned toward the parade grounds. Maybe she'd walk and try to clear her head. She stilled as she reached the flagpole and spotted at least fifty men and dogs in the center of the field.

The men barked commands, and the dogs obeyed. Instantly. Heel, and each dog nailed his shoulder to his man's knee. Sit, and the dogs promptly sat on their haunches. Stay, and the dogs waited while the men proceeded past them. Each dog had eyes only for its soldier. Lainie studied the soldiers, smiling when she saw Tom. He stood at the front of the group, his profile toward her, watching and making notes on a clipboard.

The men switched to hand commands then dropped the leashes, and the dogs continued to obey. It was an amazing sight.

"All right, men. Ten minutes to report to the obstacle course." Tom turned toward her and grinned. "Hey, Lainie. Didn't expect to see you here."

"That was fascinating. How long did it take to train the dogs to do that?"

"A couple weeks of basic training." His eyes crinkled around the corners. "You want to watch them on the obstacle course? We're going to the one across the highway today."

Excitement pumped through Lainie at the thought. "I'd love to."

"Walk with me." Tom cocked his arm, and Lainie slid her hand onto his arm.

They walked across the highway and another couple of blocks, through the gate into the war dog compound, and up a hill. Tom settled her on a rock.

"You should see everything from here. See that ridge along the dip there? That's where the dogs work. To them this is a reward for a job well done." Tom watched the gathering group of men at the obstacle course below. "Will you be okay here while I run them through their paces?"

"Yes."

In minutes, Tom had the men organized into groups. He timed the teams as they raced through the course. The dogs scrambled over bridges and into ravines, scaled rocks, and tore along the flat spots, pulling their trainers with them. Many seemed to know exactly where the finish line was, as they'd brake to a stop and grin with tongues lolling.

Lainie watched them and knew. This was it. She had to serve here.

six

May 18, 1943

Tom couldn't decide which was worse: handling the dogs himself or watching the current group of trainees manhandle the animals. For men screened for war dog training prior to shipping to Robinson, they sorely lacked an understanding of how to care for dogs.

The simple concept that you worked with a dog until he finally accomplished a task and you could reward him eluded their grasp. The poor animals were so confused, Tom didn't think they'd ever understand how to heel, let alone be successful at difficult skills such as maneuvering an obstacle course.

At this rate, eight weeks would be insufficient to get the pairs ready to ship out.

One kid from New Jersey acted as if he'd never seen a dog other than in a newsreel. Another from Alabama might have had a dog but not as a working animal. He constantly slipped human food to his dog—a bad habit if they landed in a jungle with limited food available.

The day's exercises finally ended, and Tom marched back to the barracks. He collapsed on his bed and blotted out the day. At a rap over his head, he looked up. Sid stood next to his bed.

"I'm not hungry for mess here tonight. Want to ride into Crawford and catch a bite at Mrs. Babcock's?"

Tom's mouth watered at the thought of her home cooking. Her coffee didn't taste like old socks, and the pie melted in your mouth. "Say when."

"Let me gather the rest of the guys."

Tom stood and ran a hand across his hair. It probably stood up in all directions, but he couldn't wear a hat in Mrs. Babcock's restaurant. She had strict rules about etiquette.

He pulled out a fresh shirt. His dungarees didn't look too bad, and he needed his other pairs for the balance of the week. Then he thought of Lainie. Was she still in town and at Mrs. Babcock's? He pulled on clean pants in case he saw her. A whistle pierced the long room.

"My, don't you look dandy." Sid grinned at him with Bill Byers and Dan Case looking over his shoulder. "Let's boogie while the food's still hot."

In no time they tramped up the stairs to Mrs. Babcock's and tossed their hats into the box waiting on the porch.

As Tom walked in, he searched the large room for Lainie. Her face popped into his thoughts periodically, and each time, he prayed for her. Had she found a job? Or had she returned home with her tail between her legs? He couldn't imagine her doing that willingly. No, she'd fight until forced to admit defeat.

He didn't want that to happen.

The door at the back of the room swung open, and Lainie stepped through. She'd tied an apron over her dress and scurried from table to table, refilling empty glasses with fresh milk or water. Nothing but the best for Mrs. Babcock's guests.

Guess he had the answer to his question. It looked as though she'd do anything to stay.

When her gaze landed on him, she stopped, and milk sloshed out of its container. She forced a smile on her lips. "Have a seat anywhere you like, soldiers. Mrs. Babcock will be out in a moment to help you."

"What if we'd like you?" Bill Byers leaned closer to her, clearly captured by her.

"You can always make a request, boys, but tonight my job doesn't include helping you. Better luck next time."

Despite Bill's efforts, Lainie stayed far away as Tom and the guys ate their meals. The shepherd's pie tasted as wonderful as he'd hoped, a welcome break from the fare at the mess hall. It was a good thing it was a straight shot from his plate to his mouth, because he couldn't take his eyes off her. She looked like Linda Darnell, with her dark hair falling in curls around her face. Her curls made her look soft while enhancing her natural beauty. He wondered what it would be like if she took extra care for a guy like him.

"Ask her to the USO dance Friday." Sid grinned as he poked Tom in the ribs.

"Quit mooning." Dan winked at Bill. "If you won't ask, Bill will. You know how he's always looking for a new gal to entertain."

"Yep. She's a pretty thing. I could show her a good time."

Tom grimaced at the thought of what Bill would include in that endeavor. His exploits were well known, but maybe not for a gal new to town. He had to protect her from that.

He looked up to find her standing next to him.

"More milk?"

"I'm fine." She turned to leave, but he grabbed her elbow. "Do you have any plans for Friday night?" He rushed on when she opened her mouth. Maybe he could cut off her no. "The USO's hosting a dance, and I'd be honored to escort you."

Lainie turned away from him. When he kept his hand on her elbow, she sighed and looked at him. "Look, I appreciate all your help the other day, but I can't go with you. Someone else already asked."

He released her and forced a smile. "Maybe another time."

"Maybe." She slipped away toward the kitchen.

The guys watched him intently. "Better luck next time, bud."

"Yeah. I can't say I'm surprised someone already invited her."

Tom nodded. "Some guys have all the luck. Then there are guys like me."

His voice must have carried farther than he thought, because she turned back to their table with a glint in her amber eyes. "Look, the only reason I can't go is another soldier already asked. We danced once at the North Platte Canteen, so I said yes. He said that was the best day of his enlistment. Who am I not to help? If you're there, Tom Hamilton, I'll save a dance for you." She waited until he nodded; then her shoulders eased. "I'm not so sure about the rest of you, though. You'll have to be really nice to get a dance." She winked and walked away.

Sid's pleas followed her across the room.

"Fess up, Tom. What did you do to be so favored?" Bill leaned across the table.

"Gave her a ride Friday. Seems she wants a job at Robinson."

"Remind me to volunteer to get the next shipment of dogs in Crawford." Sid knocked Tom in the shoulder.

Bill chuckled and shook his head. "All I ever get are dogs. You find a beautiful dame on your trip."

"It's not like she's overly fond of me. And we'll probably never have someone like her come to Crawford again." Tom leaned back in his chair, ears still burning from her rebuke. "Trust me, you're better off focused on one of the gals with the Women's Auxiliary Corp or the gals in Lusk."

"You know the WACs are off limits." A wicked gleam filled Dan's eyes. "Though that's only officially."

Tom leaned back in his chair as the men turned their attention from him and to stories of their escapades.

❧

Lainie leaned against the kitchen table and searched the room for any excuse to remain in the kitchen. Her hands still shook from the humiliation of those men talking about her as if she were a prize to win. Tom hadn't entered in, but he hadn't exactly protected her, either.

And why couldn't he have asked her to the dance earlier? She would have said yes, if only to avoid other offers. The men here were a little too eager to be around a pretty woman. She should have anticipated that at a fort in the middle of nowhere. Tom was different, with a noble thread she trusted.

Shame flooded her at the thought he'd caught her at this job. She hadn't wanted him to see her like this. Ever since he'd driven her to Robinson and back, her thoughts had trailed toward him. Why? He was practically a stranger. She couldn't explain it, but she cared deeply.

"Quit gathering wool and scrub these plates. I've got to use them to serve that new table of folks." Esther swiped her arm across her forehead, smearing the sweat around. "I don't know why everyone decided tonight was the night to grace us with their presence. I've only got one shepherd's pie left. Hope it's enough. I've never run out of food." She threw plates on a tray and hurried back toward the dining room.

Lainie glared at the sink full of suds and dishes. Her hands would never be soft again after all the time she spent with her hands dunked in the burning water. Mama would be horrified, but Mama couldn't stop her. And Lainie had come to like her little room. She wouldn't leave until she had a job here and had made her way. If that meant washing dishes by the sink load, she'd do it. She dove into the pile of dishes with a sudsy rag.

She hummed a hymn as she worked. "It is well with my soul." The words filled her mind with peace and replaced the tightness around her heart. She continued to hum and pondered the words.

Could it be well with her soul when everything around her had fallen apart? Her dream of serving in Europe lay in ashes around her feet. Her health still hadn't recovered, though she had more good days now. She didn't have the job she needed. . . yet. But peace flooded her heart.

She longed for a way to bottle the feeling, to seal it in her heart for those moments when the fear and disappointment overwhelmed her. Elbow-deep in the water, she sang the words until they saturated her heart: "It is well with my soul. It is well, it is well with my soul."

seven

May 21, 1943

Strains of a Benny Goodman number ricocheted around the Recreation Building. Tom grimaced as the clarinetist with the post orchestra hit a sour note. Though the group got better with each performance, rough spots remained. The notes didn't appear to bother anyone already dancing.

He glanced around the room and noted the soldiers lining the walls. A group of pretty ladies and their chaperones congregated near the punch bowl. He could walk over and ask one of them to swing. Instead, he joined John and Naomi Tyler in a corner.

"Why aren't you two dancing?"

Naomi giggled and looked at John with eyes filled with adoration. "We've already danced until I was breathless."

"You missed the Charleston, Tom. We really cut up the floor."

The image of gangly John swinging his arms and legs in the Charleston filled Tom's mind. "Now that's a scene I'm not sorry to miss."

"I'm not that bad." John looked Tom over. "We can have a contest sometime if you like. See who Charlestons better."

"No thanks. Those arms and legs of yours are long enough to hurt someone. You need some kind of warning system."

"Har, har, Hamilton." John looked across the hall. "Isn't that the dame you gave a ride?"

"Yes, that's her."

Lainie breezed by in the arms of some private with the remount unit.

"Mrs. Babcock introduced us on Saturday. I hear she's

44

looking for a job." Naomi's words gushed out. "She seems nice enough."

"She is, with a sharp wit. She'll tell you exactly what she thinks."

"Nothing wrong with that." Naomi frowned at him and crossed her arms. "Don't you need more help in the war dogs office?"

"Not in my area, right, John?"

John shook his head and grinned. "Don't look to me for help, Hamilton. You know how Naomi gets when she has an idea. Might as well agree to help and save yourself a lot of misery."

What would it be like to enjoy Miss Gardner's sparks on a daily basis? The question intrigued him. She got even more adorable when her eyes lit up in a challenge. And he loved a good challenge. First, he had to get her to look at him. Without rolling her eyes or spouting off.

"Well, I'll collect that dance she promised me."

John grabbed Naomi and spun her around. "Sounds like a good idea. Let's swing, honey."

Naomi giggled in delight. Two bright spots of color bloomed on her cheeks. Watching the two of them, Tom longed for the same type of relationship with a woman. One tailor-made for him.

Lainie whizzed by in the arms of another soldier. This time it looked as though panic caused the color on her cheeks. She kept pushing space between her and the soldier, only to have him yank her closer again. Tom watched for another moment then stepped onto the floor. In a few steps, he caught up with the couple.

"Excuse me, but I believe you owe me a dance, Miss Gardner."

Lainie looked at him with a tight smile. "You are correct. Soldier, I'm afraid our dance will have to be cut short." She tried again to pull away from her partner.

"You heard her."

The private grimaced at Tom. "You can dance after the song ends."

"You can't force her to continue." As Tom tried to decide how to handle the situation without it exploding into a brawl, Lainie raised her foot and brought her heel down on the man's shoe. He howled and hopped on the other foot.

"Thank you for the dance. Please lead on, Tom."

"It would be an honor." He pulled her slight body into the circle of his arms and began to sway to the music. As he held her, his senses went on high alert. He could smell Lainie's flowery perfume. The movements of couples around them faded away until all he saw was Lainie.

&

Lainie took a deep breath. When that didn't calm her racing pulse, she took another. That last soldier had rattled her with his insistence that she dance close to him. Now as she whirled with Tom, she felt sheltered, protected even. There was nothing pushy about the way he guided her around the floor. Far from a clod with two left feet, he led her through the dance with grace.

"Thank you." Her words whispered into his collar.

"For what?"

"Rescuing me from that boor." She tipped her chin up so she could see his eyes. Tonight they looked like they could be green or blue. A mystery mix of color and emotion. "So where's your date, Tom? I'm sure she's not happy you're with me right now."

"Why would you say that?"

"I seem to have that effect on women. They see me as competition rather than as friend material. Something of a Scarlett O'Hara, I'm afraid."

"You're blunt, aren't you?"

"And you ask lots of questions."

Tom laughed, and Lainie decided she liked the sound. "You don't laugh much, do you?"

"Turning the tables on me?"

"As often as I can. It's part of my charm."

"You seem to have an abundance of that."

"My mama taught me well."

Tom guffawed, and Lainie smiled in delight.

"To answer your question, I came alone." Tom smiled down at her, and she decided his eyes were definitely a soft blue like the sky on a clear summer day. She could search their depths for a long time and see only a small fraction of his soul.

"You are not a simple man, Specialist Hamilton."

"Nope. My daddy didn't raise a fool. He thought I should be a Renaissance man."

"All while living in Wyoming." Lainie followed his steady lead as the band continued to play.

"Not everyone can be fortunate enough to live in that great state. The land is filled with big sky."

"From what I've heard, there's not much else. Frankly, it doesn't sound much different from here."

"Maybe that's why I like Fort Robinson. There's the same sense of wide-open space. A man isn't crowded. There's plenty of air to breathe and land to roam on the back of a horse."

"So you have the heart of a cowboy?"

"First you tell me I'm a preacher, now a cowboy." Tom shook his head.

Tom's dance steps slowed as the clarinet wailed the last notes of the song. Lainie quirked an eyebrow at him when he stepped back.

"Thanks for the dance, Lainie. I won't monopolize your time tonight."

The first spark of temper ignited at his words. Had she missed something? They'd been in the middle of an amusing conversation, and now he backed away? She turned without a word and flounced away. Two could play that game. She didn't look over her shoulder even when she felt his gaze.

A corporal jostled against Lainie. She stepped back and landed against the wall.

"Excuse me, Miss. . ." He let the last word carry as if waiting for her to fill in a blank.

Instead, she nodded to him then sidestepped toward the refreshment table. She'd had her fill of uniforms for one night. Tom's abrupt dismissal had ended the night on a sour note. She knew she should shake it off and let the corporal dance with her. Fatigue weighed her down, and she didn't have the energy to pretend she cared about another dance.

Out of all the soldiers she'd danced with, only one had proven worthy of her sparring. And he'd abandoned her after one wonderful dance.

The room closed in on her, so she left. Once she reached the outside of the building, the sounds of the orchestra faded away. In the growing stillness of the night, she looked at the sky and gaped at the infinite number of stars glowing against the inky sky.

"It's breathtaking, isn't it?"

Lainie jumped and turned to see Tom standing to her side. "Don't you ever announce yourself?"

"Didn't want to ruin the moment."

"Like scaring the life out of a girl doesn't accomplish that." She took a deep breath and turned back to the sky. "It is amazing."

"God must delight in creating. Think about each of those stars, and there must be more that we can't see."

"You're in preacher mode?"

His white teeth shone in the darkness as he smiled. "I guess I am. There's something about the vastness of creation that turns my thoughts to the Creator. Clear nights like tonight make it easy." He looked at her for a long moment, and Lainie couldn't break from his gaze. "Do you have a ride back to Mrs. Babcock's?"

"No, I didn't think about when the shuttle would run back."

"You don't plan much, do you?"

She turned on him, back stiff and chin raised high. "I thought I'd ask someone else who had to go back to Crawford for a ride."

"Does this someone have a name?"

"No. But that doesn't mean I'm stranded."

"Maybe, but walking isn't a great idea in the dark."

"Thanks for the words of wisdom. I'll be sure to keep them in mind." She shrugged. "Besides, my shoes'll never recover from my last attempt."

Tom took a deep breath and exhaled it as if he were blowing out a candle. Lainie waited, foot tapping, for the next barrage of words. "Come on, spit it out."

"What?"

"That you think I'm a fool and never should have come. That the town and fort would be better off with me at home being spoiled by a daddy who's overprotective. That I shouldn't expect to do anything more than be coddled the rest of my days. And that I'll die of boredom, but that's my lot in life." Lainie ran out of breath and sputtered to a stop.

Tom shook his head. "You misunderstood. While I like to have a plan, that doesn't mean you should go home. Let me give you a ride. I'll rest better knowing you're safely home."

"Okay." Lainie relaxed her shoulders and smiled. "Maybe we can last those few minutes without annoying each other."

"I sincerely doubt that. My car's over here." Tom settled her in his black Chevy coupe and pointed the car down the highway.

Lainie gazed out the window at the stars pinpointing the sky like a million twinkling night-lights. In no time, Tom pulled the car to a stop in front of Mrs. Babcock's. He hopped out and opened her door.

"Here you go." He offered her his hand and helped her from the car.

She found herself next to him again, could feel the warmth he radiated surround her. She drew a steadying breath but couldn't move. He tipped her chin up with his finger. The action sent a jolt through her, making her aware of every detail. The fragrance of lilacs hung in the air, and a slight breeze chilled her skin. His gaze slipped from her eyes to her lips, and she stilled.

The screen door slammed, and Lainie jumped. "I should go in."

"Join me for a walk after church? I'll give you a tour of the fort."

"Okay. See you Sunday." Lainie floated to her room, wondering what his kiss would have felt like. She could only imagine.

eight

May 23, 1943

Lainie slid into the pew at First Christian Church next to Esther. She wondered if Tom would attend services here or if he'd come for her later. She'd spent yesterday wondering how he'd find her then decided she'd have a hard time hiding in a town this size.

The organist played the opening notes to "Amazing Grace," and Lainie tried to settle her thoughts. She couldn't help that they continually wandered to a man who raised her blood pressure faster than anyone else could. But his innate kindness also set him apart from other men.

The service passed in a blur as Pastor Stevenson focused on Isaiah 43. "Read with me. 'But now, this is what the Lord says—he who created you, O Jacob, he who formed you, O Israel: "Fear not, for I have redeemed you; I have summoned you by name; you are mine. When you pass through the waters, I will be with you; and when you pass through the rivers, they will not sweep over you."'"

If that was true, then where was God when she'd been so sick? She'd cried out but had felt so incredibly alone in Kentucky with no one to care what happened to her. Her mom had planned to make a quick trip until Lainie's father had decided her illness wasn't life-threatening. The memory of that isolation overwhelmed her, and she shivered. She would do everything she could to avoid that feeling again.

The pastor's voice rose and pulled her attention back to his words. " 'Since you are precious and honored in my sight, and because I love you, I will give men in exchange for you, and people in exchange for your life. Do not be afraid, for I am

51

with you.'" If He'd truly been with her, why had her dreams of serving as a nurse been crushed? Hadn't that been a good thing for her to do? If it wasn't going to happen, why hadn't God prevented her from wasting so much time in training?

People around her stood, and Lainie looked up to find them holding hymnbooks. Somehow she'd missed the last twenty minutes of the service, trapped by the questions swirling in her mind. Esther poked her in the side and frowned at her, her hat feather bobbing and dipping. Lainie stood and glanced around the sanctuary for Tom. Her heart sank when she didn't see him. She opened the hymnal and sang with the congregation.

After the benediction and dismissal, Lainie slipped from the pew and dashed to the entrance. Her mind spun. The words from Isaiah couldn't apply to her. She certainly didn't feel precious in God's sight. No, ignored or overlooked fit better.

She gasped for air as she hit the sidewalk.

"Are you okay?"

She looked up to find Tom leaning against his black Chevy in front of the church. She drew a shaky breath and pasted on a smile. "I see you found me."

"Not a difficult task. Everyone knows which church Mrs. Babcock attends. I figured you'd join her."

"Good guesswork, soldier." Feeling less shaky, she forced the questions from her mind and approached him. She tilted her head to catch his gaze. "I believe you owe me a tour."

He opened the passenger door for her. "Your chariot awaits."

He settled her in the seat then hustled around the car. In moments, they headed toward the highway and then the fort. Lainie breathed deeply and watched the landscape fly past. She turned toward Tom and considered him. His strong profile hinted at his steadiness. Nothing rattled him, and if anything did, he'd approach it with steady steps and a clear head.

He glanced her way and arched an eyebrow. "What?"

She ducked and felt heat climb her cheeks. She tried to cover the smile that pushed up her cheeks.

"It can't be that bad."

"You look like an unshakable rock."

His shoulders shook, and he pulled his hat low over his eyes.

"Hey. You're the one who asked."

"I suppose I did. I'm a touch scared to hear the next label you'll slap on me. Cowboy. Heartthrob."

She playfully slapped him on the shoulder. "Stop it. And don't think for a minute that I'll answer your question the next time you ask."

"Duly noted." He slowed his car and pulled to a stop in front of a white concrete pad with posts.

"What's this?"

"The post swimming pool. But we're headed to the war dog area. Those buildings on either side of the pool are barracks. And there are a few barns to the right. But over here to the left is my world."

Lainie hurried to follow him from the car and match his stride. She had to double-time to keep up. She pulled to a stop after a few minutes. "Tom, if you really want to show me, you need to either slow down or carry me."

He sized her up as though he thought she seriously wanted him to haul her around. She waved her arms and backed up. "That's a figure of speech. I'm shorter than you, and this isn't a race."

A sheepish grin covered his face, and he rubbed his neck. "Right. Sorry about that, Lainie."

She lingered over the way her name rolled off his tongue. She could get used to hearing that. He gazed at her so long she realized she looked rude. "You must love your dogs."

He frowned at her. "Why would you say that?"

"You're so eager to show them to me."

"I'd rather work with one hundred stubborn mules than ten dogs." He rubbed a scar that ran the length of his hand.

"Maybe, but you're sprinting toward the dogs."

"True." He cocked his elbow and, once she accepted it, stepped forward in mincing steps. "This better?"

"Much." His arm felt solid beneath her fingers. She drew in a deep breath and inhaled the clean air. "You know what I miss? The flowers and trees that scent the air with spring. Out here, you can't smell any of that."

"Watering plants isn't a high government priority. You'll grow fond of the prairie grass." They crested a shallow hill, and Lainie stopped walking. A small compound of buildings stretched before them. "To the left stand the administrative buildings. Farther up the hill, do you see that small brick building?"

Lainie nodded. It looked more like a shed than a usable space.

"We store fireworks and arms there."

She looked from the building to him. "Why would you have that here with the dogs?"

"We use the fireworks to prepare them for what they'll hear if they're sent to the front."

She shivered at the thought of a dog like her family's undergoing that stress. Poor Mason spent each thunderstorm dashing from window to window in an effort to protect the house. She calmed only when the thunder ended.

"Over to the right is the main receiving building and the hospital. We can handle about eighty dogs at a time there." Tom led her up a winding road to the top of another hill. The arms shed now stood immediately to their left, and in front of them spread a plain with a track running in a loose oval around the perimeter, and the highway beyond that. A large pond stood to the right with a fence around it.

"What's the fence for?"

"The colonel ordered it up after Pearl Harbor. Somebody decided the only thing saboteurs would want to attack is our water source." He spoke louder to be heard over the growing din.

Lainie turned to search for the source of the sound.

"Look over to your right."

She followed his arm, and her eyes widened. Row after

row of wooden six-by-six boxes lined an open field. A line of trees separated another field from the first. "How many dogs are out there?"

"Somewhere around eighteen hundred. They come and go in waves. Most will be here for training eight to twelve weeks. And they may be here a few weeks before we match them with a trainer."

As she listened to Tom, Lainie wandered closer to the first row of dogs. A beautiful collie sat in the shadow of the first hut. She knelt in front of it and reached out to stroke its coat.

"What are you doing?" Panic laced Tom's voice. He yanked her away from the animal before she could answer.

She slapped his grasp away. "What? I only wanted to pet the dog. She's gorgeous."

"Lainie, you can't do that. We train these animals to be war dogs. Not pets. You don't know if that dog has had aggression training. It could attack simply because it's trained to." He took a deep breath and looked at her with eyes darkened by emotion. "You must treat each dog like it's dangerous." He hustled her back to the car.

The air between them crackled. If he was so afraid, why work with dogs? She wanted to ask, but he wouldn't stop talking long enough. The tour turned into a preemptory one of the fort's main compound after that. She sighed in relief when he finally dropped her back at Esther's.

⁂

Monday morning, Lainie helped with the morning chores before settling into a rocker on the wide front porch. She watched the world ease by and wondered what she should do. She needed a strategy beyond washing dishes and typing nonsense. Something had to happen soon.

The screen door opened, and Esther stepped out with her hat on and bag in hand. "What are you sitting there for? It's time to find you a job."

Lainie jumped from the chair and grabbed the hat and bag Esther handed her. She had to smile at the way Esther hurried down the stairs and down the sidewalk without a glance back. "What do you have in mind?"

"There are a few more folks for you to meet. And Mary Nelson told me yesterday there might be an opening with the war dogs. You were too busy talking to Tom to hear."

Lainie considered protesting but decided it wasn't worth the breath. Esther had her mind made up. In one short week, Lainie had learned there was no point in trying to change Esther's opinions. They strolled downtown, and soon Esther had reintroduced Lainie to half of the business owners. Even with Esther's endorsement, the shops didn't need help.

"Mary said she'd meet us at Mae's for lunch." Esther waited for a passing soldier to open the door and then entered.

Lainie smiled at the sergeant and tilted her chin before following. She glanced around the diner for Mary, taking in the details she'd missed last time. The inside was small with a handful of tables scattered across a worn linoleum floor. Faded Coca-Cola wallpaper lined the walls. The scent of old grease hung in the air, mixing with the sweetness of ice cream and candy. Lainie closed her eyes and imagined she'd been transported back to Wahl's Drugstore in North Platte to share a cherry Coke with Audrey.

"Are you going to sit down?"

Lainie opened her eyes and frowned. She was very much in Mae's and not Wahl's. Esther smiled at her from the corner table.

"Have a seat. I'm sure Mary will be here momentarily." Esther peeled off her gloves and placed them on the table.

Lainie pulled back the chair and sat. "Do you think I should stay?"

"I think you need to wait until you've given this a fair chance. Did I ever tell you why I run a restaurant? I don't need to, you know." A faraway look settled in Esther's eyes. "My father paid off the mortgage and left the house to me free and clear. I thought about selling and going to a new town after my husband died. Start a new life somewhere and do something important. Something that really mattered. Well, twenty years later, I'm still here, and it's exactly where I'm supposed to be."

"How can you know?" Lainie yearned for that assurance.

Esther looked at her and smiled. "Each of those boys who walks through my door looking for a smile and a slice of homemade pie brings an opportunity to minister and serve. I can't think of many other places where I could mother so many boys at one time. They're good men, but many of them are on their own for the first time. And many never imagined they'd spend time in a little place like Crawford. Each time I serve a slice of pie, I pray for the man receiving it. And that's enough."

"But why help me?"

"Because it's been placed on my heart to help you." She leaned across the table and touched Lainie's hand. Comfort flowed through her touch to Lainie. "You're like a little bird that's lost its way. And I'm here to help you find it."

The door burst open, and Mary rushed in. "Oh, I hope you didn't wait long." The words babbled from her mouth in a rush that made Lainie wonder how she took a breath. "But, Mrs. Babcock, I think you'll be pleased. Oh, I hope you will be."

nine

May 24, 1943

Monday morning flew by in the routine of tending the dogs. Tom rubbed his scar and cringed at the memory of his reaction when Lainie had reached out to the collie. She'd have been fine with that animal, but other dogs were a different story. He'd overreacted but wouldn't change it. She had to understand the kind of animals that were out here before she got hurt.

He wished the air hadn't changed between them. One moment, it had been the best afternoon of his life as he showed her pieces of his world. The next, she looked at him as if he'd gone insane.

It wasn't insanity. Not really. And someday he'd find a way to make her understand what it was like to confront your fear on a daily basis and pray God would remove the fear or the job.

Well, today that prayer was partly answered. He'd work with the dogs only half days for the next six weeks. Basic training had arrived at Fort Robinson, and it was his turn to experience the joys.

John Tyler stomped through the door of the war dog training building. "Can you believe we get to play soldier today?"

Tom grinned at his words. "If you haven't noticed, we are soldiers."

"Yeah, but we've never been that kind of soldier. Why do I need hand-to-hand combat training when I'm stationed here? I mean, what's the army going to do? Ship me overseas?" His eyes bugged, and he shook his head. "You don't think they'd send me out?"

"Well, you are a member of the quartermaster corp. I suppose anything's possible."

"Don't tell Naomi. She'd pass out."

Tom got up from the desk and jostled John. "I'm afraid you should have thought about this before you enlisted."

"But that's exactly why I enlisted here. You come here when you want to work with animals and stay in the boondocks." John swallowed so hard that his Adam's apple bobbed up and down. He wiped beads of sweat from his forehead and took half a step toward the door. Tom grabbed him before he could bolt.

"Don't do anything crazy. Let's just get through this and then worry about what's next. At least they aren't shipping us out for the training. And I don't mind the break from our regular duty. We might even learn something interesting."

John nodded slowly. "Anything's possible."

Tom reached for his Daisy Mae hat and shoved it on his head. Time to get John moving. "Come on; they'll be looking for us if we don't head out."

Together they hiked across the highway and over to the field that had been designated for basic training. Tom had talked to some of the guys who'd gone through the first round of training. It didn't sound too rigorous. Some shooting, some marching, some hand-to-hand combat. Maybe a little book learning, but not much.

At the first words from Master Sergeant Maxwell, Tom wondered if the men he'd talked to had actually experienced basic training. If so, they must have had a different instructor. Sergeant Maxwell seemed determined to beat them into soldiers in an afternoon. Push-ups, running miles in boots, and endless lectures weren't enough. Tom couldn't wait to collapse in the barracks; Sergeant made them march in formation around and around the post parade grounds until Tom was dizzy. Finally, the sergeant released them.

Tom plopped on the ground. "Day one down. Do you think the others will be like this?"

"Probably." A hangdog look dragged John's face to the ground. "Guess I'll head to town."

"We still have our regular afternoon duties with the dogs." Sid panted as he collapsed alongside Tom on the ground.

John and Tom looked at each other and groaned.

"You're kidding, right?" Tom waited for Sid to give any indication it had been a joke. "No one mentioned that to us."

"Welcome to the real army, Hamilton."

Fatigue washed over Tom in a wave at the thought of hours of work caring for the animals. Slowly, he stood. "Maybe today was designed to test our mettle. Let's go, John."

❧

The week slogged by in a monotonous routine. The days developed a cadence that pushed Tom through each activity. He spent the mornings instructing the new handlers in the care of their dogs. Even the most mundane activities such as checking for ticks seemed strange to some of the city boys. Once they started exercises in the field, its importance would become clear.

Afternoons, he struggled through basic training exercises. He'd always expected to receive orders to ship out. Some of his friends got those exact orders—a few headed east to Europe, others west. Now that he knew the skills the army deemed important to its soldiers, his duties at the fort took on a whole new light.

He'd heard stories that the initial group of soldiers who'd shipped out with dogs had told about combat in the Far East. He could imagine the brutality of war from the headlines and from stories he'd heard from his uncles about the Great War.

But now. . .now he wondered how he would behave in combat. Sometimes he dreamed about being the hero, but here he knew what was expected of him and that he could perform his tasks well even if reluctantly. He wanted to think his fear had abandoned him. Then he considered donning the pads required for aggression training and wanted to flee post quicker than a pheasant running across the road.

Ready or not, each day of basic training got him closer to shipping out.

"Hey there, soldier."

A perky voice pulled him from his thoughts. He looked up to see Lainie Gardner walking across the war dog area toward him. "What brings you to my neck of the woods?"

"A job." Her smile reached her eyes for the first time since he'd met her. The joy in her eyes knocked the breath from him, and he had to remind his lungs to inhale.

"That's great news. Where are you stationed?"

"Right here." She shrugged and nodded toward the office building. "I get to type responses to the letters families send. I'll probably draft honorable discharge papers soon. Who would have thought dogs could receive that honor?"

"It seemed fitting when we sent the first dogs home."

"Clever. I'm sure the families appreciate it." She cocked her head and looked up at him. "Walk with me?"

He nodded and matched his stride to hers.

"I thought I'd see you more." Lainie pouted and then stumbled. He offered his arm to steady her.

"Basic training's in full swing. I'm running every direction right now." Tom looked at her hand resting on his arm, her fingers delicate against his rough uniform.

"Seems a little backward to me, taking basic training a year after you enlisted."

Tom shrugged. Lainie didn't seem to be headed anywhere in particular. "Can I escort you somewhere? I need to get back to my duties before Sarge looks for me."

"Will you come to Mrs. Babcock's for dessert tonight? She plans to bake pear pies."

"I can't say I've ever had that kind of pie, but I'll try to come."

"Good." She nodded her head, and her straw hat bobbed with the action. She reached up and tugged it back in place. "I'll see you then."

Lainie stepped away and headed toward the office. She looked back over her shoulder at him, and he grinned. She was something else. As he watched, another soldier approached her, and she smiled up at him. Whatever she said to him caused him to laugh, and Tom frowned. She flirted with all the boys. He shouldn't feel flattered by her attention. Instead, he wouldn't be surprised if he found Mrs. Babcock's filled with a dozen soldiers surrounding Lainie.

Well, he'd kept both of his sisters out of trouble with their beaus. He could do the same for her. It looked as though she'd need it.

He managed to slip away after mess and took Sid with him. Tom was surprised to find the street empty of extra cars when they pulled up to Mrs. Babcock's. Maybe his assumption had missed the mark.

Sid and Tom clomped up the stairs, tossed their hats in the box, and knocked on the front door.

"Good evening, boys." Mrs. Babcock smiled at them in her motherly way and ushered them to the dining room. "Sit down over here. I'll be out in a minute with some pie and fresh coffee. How's that extra training?"

"Just fine, ma'am. Thank you." Tom settled into a chair at the table she'd pointed to. The radio played swing music in the background. Sounded like WLW out of Chicago playing the latest from Duke Ellington.

Sid sank into another chair. "I thought others would be here."

"Guess not."

Someone clacked across the wood floor, and Tom looked up expecting to see Mrs. Babcock with her tray of goodies. Instead, Lainie stepped into view. She was wearing a fresh green dress that brought sparks to her eyes. She'd swept her hair off her shoulders.

She smiled at him then included Sid in her smile. "Glad you boys could join us. I knew I'd need help eating all this pie."

She sat down, and in a moment, Mrs. Babcock joined them.

Another boarder or two filtered down, probably attracted by the sound of their laughter. Mrs. Babcock grabbed a deck of cards from the stack of games in the corner, and they played a round of canasta. Tom relaxed the longer they played. Lainie seemed to have lost her airs and settled into an evening of pure fun. He could get used to nights like this. No pressure, just fun.

ten

Thursday morning, Lainie breezed into the K-9 Office. She'd worn her link-button worsted suit and felt smart in it. The gray offset her dark curls, which she'd worn loose. She felt prepared to tackle the day.

"Good morning, Mary."

Mary Nelson sat behind her battered wooden desk that looked as if it had first seen service during the late 1800s. Five more desks filled the center of the office space. The walls were lined with equally beat-up metal file cabinets. Lainie glanced around but didn't see the others in the office.

"Are we it?"

"Today. The others are in Chadron for training. Don't worry; they'll liven things up when they return."

Lainie plopped her veiled beret on the coat tree tucked behind the door. Then she settled into her desk and looked at the stack of waiting papers. Her first assignment was creating a file for each dog that pranced through the gate of the War Dog Training Compound.

Turning, she noticed how quiet Mary was. "Are you okay?"

Mary shrank behind her desk and shook her head. A tear trickled down her cheek, and Lainie hurried over and crouched beside her. "Tell me what's wrong. Please, Mary."

Mary shrugged and then turned away while swiping a handkerchief across her cheeks. "I'll be okay."

"You don't look it."

A moan leaked between Mary's lips. Lainie's gaze fell to the desk, and she stilled. A shredded Western Union envelope and crumpled telegram sat on the desktop. She'd heard about so many of those telegrams that she didn't think her heart could hurt for the families and loved ones who received them. She'd been wrong.

She hugged Mary and rocked her. After a moment, Mary straightened and inhaled around a shuddering sob.

"Who was he?"

"Philip Tucker." Mary twisted a ring on her left hand. "We were supposed to marry during his last furlough, but he decided to wait until he returned from the war. He didn't want me to be a widow." Fresh sobs cut off her words.

Lainie hugged her and prayed for the right words. Nothing came to her that didn't seem trite, so she stayed quiet. *Why do so many have to suffer like this, Lord?*

Mary tried to sit up, a watery smile pasted on her face. She picked up the telegram and smoothed out the wrinkles. Lainie looked at her and renewed her vow not to fall for a man in uniform. She'd spend time with them and enjoy their company. But she couldn't invite the pain Mary and so many others had experienced since the war started.

"Can you take today off?"

Mary nodded. Lainie assisted her to stand then watched helplessly as Mary retrieved her jacket and headed out the door. "Please let me know if you need anything."

After Mary left, Lainie wandered around the small office, considering the stacks of papers waiting to be filed. Suddenly it didn't seem so important that she had a job at a military post. The longing to be on her way to the fight overwhelmed her. She sank into a chair and covered her face with her hands. *I'll never understand, God. Why did You have to kill that dream?*

She heard the door squeak on its hinges and squared her shoulders. Corporal Hutchinson stalked into the room.

"Where's Miss Nelson?"

"She just received word her fiancé died. Can I help you?"

He slapped a stack of papers on the corner of her desk. "Here's the next round of discharges to be processed."

She fought a groan at the paperwork that multiplied in all directions. If she didn't get to work, she'd be buried under the mess, and it would take weeks for them to find her body.

"Yes, sir." She picked up the first pile.

The morning passed with Lainie's thoughts returning to Mary and her grief. War wounded so many more than those who served. One stack filed, she grabbed the discharges and sat at her desk. She stared at the typewriter and prayed all those hours of practice had paid off. Otherwise, she'd be out of a job before she saw her first paycheck.

"Here goes." She slipped a form into the back of the type-writer and rolled it until it curved toward her. She played with the levers until the page lined up properly. Looking at the order, her gaze darted back and forth as she hunted out each letter in the dog's name. "Sebastian. What happened to short names like Mutt?"

She muttered her way through two crumpled attempts.

"Do you always talk to yourself?"

Lainie jumped and looked up to see a soldier standing in the doorway with easy, Clark Gable elegance. She released a breath and fisted her hands on her hips. "You should announce yourself."

"Second Lieutenant Brian Daniels at your service."

"Then hop behind that typewriter and get to work. I'm sure you can tell I need all the help I can get."

"Let me take you to lunch."

"Why would I do that when I'm so successful here? The work's simply evaporating."

"Maybe the break would make you more accurate. Your fingers must be starved for nourishment. That I can help with."

She scrutinized the soldier from his hat, which looked freshly brushed, down to the tips of his polished boots. "You're visiting."

"How could you tell?"

"Few soldiers look that spit and polished after a few hours' work. If you haven't noticed, it's dry and dusty."

"I'm here to inspect the war dog center. And I'm sure in my orders I'll find one about taking the starving clerical pool to lunch."

Lainie threw her arms in the air. "You win."

She stood and accepted the lieutenant's proffered arm. A look of satisfaction settled on his face, and he steered her out of the cramped office. As a female civilian, Lainie could join the WACs for their meals or bring her own. The lieutenant took her to the officers' mess instead.

The aroma of Italian spices permeated the air. Lasagna that tasted almost like Mama's filled Lainie's plate, and she inhaled it. In between bites, she asked Brian questions about his life back home. He regaled her with tales of growing up in Maine and the culture shock he'd received upon enlisting.

"You can just imagine this small-town boy from Nowhere, Maine, being berated by a drill sergeant from the Bronx. I could hardly understand a word he said. And no matter what he said, my answer was the wrong one."

Lainie smiled at the familiar story. The war had a way of mixing men who'd never meet under normal circumstances.

Their dinner was interrupted several times by other officers stopping long enough to introduce themselves. Her mind swam with names and ranks before the rich cheesecake arrived.

She glanced at her watch and gasped. "Thank you for lunch, but I have to get back."

"Can I see you again while I'm here?" Brian stared intently at her as if memorizing every detail of her face.

Heat climbed her cheeks, but she refused to look away. "I suppose. Though I won't have time for two-hour lunches every day." He stood to escort her back, but she waved him down. "I'm sure you have other things to do. I'll walk alone the block or two back to my post. Thanks for a delightful lunch."

She strolled back to the office, searching the face of each soldier she passed and smiling at them. It wasn't until she reached her building that she realized she'd looked for Tom the whole time. He'd looked worn last night but had relaxed and shown a competitive streak as tall as the buttes once the game got under way. She hadn't laughed that hard in a long time, and it felt good even as her sides ached.

She entered the office and smiled to see another warm body. "Liz, right?"

"Yes, ma'am. Liz Czaplewski at your service. Don't worry; my last name is not required to get my attention."

"That's good, since it's a tongue twister. Glad to have company."

In minutes, they settled into a routine that had Lainie far from the typewriter and her aborted attempts to complete the paperwork. By the end of the day, the office looked like a different place.

"This is why I love to float. I get to come into the middle of chaos and transform it."

Lainie had to agree. The to-be-filed piles had shrunk to fill the top of one desk. Liz had dealt with the stack of discharge papers effortlessly. Not one had been crumpled and thrown to the ground. Lainie shook her head at the thought of all the practice she'd need before she mirrored that competency.

Waiting for the shuttle, Lainie realized she'd made an important advancement that day. She felt connected to a couple of the women in town in a way that held the promise of friendship. Add Esther to the mix, and Crawford just might come to feel like home someday. Hope sparked in her at the thought.

A wolf whistle brought her back to the ground. She turned to find the soldier and shook her finger at him with a playful grin. The soldier placed his hands over his heart and swooned. Boys. It didn't matter which corner of the country they were in. They all acted the same around pretty girls. Lainie's smile widened. She was definitely in the right place.

Other soldiers took up the call, and she refused to look around to find the sources. If the bus didn't arrive soon, she might strike out on her own. Slowly the voices died down, and she looked back toward the soldiers. The lieutenant from lunch approached with a steady stride.

"Looks like you could use some protection while you wait."

Lainie nodded. "They're good boys."

"Not used to a beautiful woman like you standing unescorted." He squeezed her hand where it rested on his arm. "Don't worry. I'll take good care of you."

Lainie considered him carefully and wondered what he really meant. Part of her felt relief at his words. The other part detected an undercurrent she didn't understand.

eleven

"You're dismissed."

With those words, Tom spun toward the barracks. He had an A pass in his back pocket and could taste the freedom of a couple of days without demands. After this week, he needed the break.

"Heading to Lusk this weekend, Hamilton?" Sarge Lewis joined Tom.

"No, think I'll stick closer to base."

The sarge nodded. "Good work this week. You'll complete basic in seven weeks, and life'll return to normal. At least for the quartermasters."

"Yes, sir."

"Keep it up." Sarge ambled off, and Tom shook his head. The exchange had a surreal feel to it. Where was the bark and bite Sarge prided himself on?

After a quick shower, Tom felt like a new man. Sid and Bill Byers entered the barracks, both looking a little wet around the ears. Lucky Bill had endured basic training before Robinson, so he'd spent the week filling gaps left by the men in training. Sid looked as wrung out as Tom felt. Yep, the three would light Crawford up tonight. They'd settled on the pavilion dance in the park rather than travel to Chadron, Alliance, or Lusk.

Sid plopped beside Tom on his cot. "Time's wasting if we want a real meal before the dance."

They hurried out to Tom's '41 Chevy and hopped in. He revved the engine through the bends in the highway and slowed only when they hit the gas station that signaled the beginning of Crawford. "Where to, fellows?"

"Well, there's Babcock's." Bill licked his lips as he rapped his hand against the window frame in time to the strains of "Don't Get Around Much Anymore."

Sid shook his head. "Already had pie there this week."

"That doesn't leave many options. We can always head back and inhale the wonderful grub at the mess hall." Tom looked away from the road long enough to grin at the other two.

"Yep. I mean nope." Bill shrugged. "Mrs. Babcock's it is."

Sid nodded enthusiastically. "Maybe some of the gals would like a ride to the dance."

"Always looking for the positive, aren't you?" Tom stopped in front of Mrs. Babcock's and hopped out. He opened the door, looking for a little gal with dark hair and sparkling eyes. He stopped short. He had no right or reason to look for Lainie Gardner. Bill plowed into him, and he jerked forward.

"Come on; I hope we aren't too late for her stew." Bill bolted to a table and plopped into the closest chair. The tablecloth slid across the table into his lap, a candle wobbling precariously. Bill steadied it.

"Slow down. You know she'll have something for us." Sid looked around the room. "It's a hopping place tonight."

A buzz rose from the tables surrounding them and formed a backdrop as Tom settled in. At most tables, couples stared deeply into each other's eyes, with a few filled with soldiers he recognized from the post. Ellen, Mrs. Babcock's regular waitress, waltzed to their table with her order pad in hand.

"What can I get you fellas tonight? The special is country fried steak with all the fixings." She disappeared into the kitchen with three orders for the special. In a moment, she returned with mugs of iced tea. She winked at Tom as she slapped them on the table. "Courtesy of Esther."

Sid groaned and picked up his mug. "This isn't exactly what I had in mind when I imagined holding a cold mug."

"Yeah, but you'll enjoy the night a whole lot more."

"Might even remember it," Bill said with a snicker.

The meal tasted better than Tom had hoped, with Sid and Bill joking back and forth with a neighboring table. The gals boarded with Mrs. Babcock and enjoyed the banter. Tom couldn't help noticing who wasn't at that table. "Hey, Ellen, is Lainie Gardner here tonight?"

"No. Some lieutenant picked her up earlier. Think they're headed to the dance later."

For some reason, his stomach twisted at the thought. "Thanks."

"Trouble in paradise?" Sid grinned across the table at him.

Tom rolled his eyes. "You know better than that. Found someone to take to the dance?"

"Absolutely. These two beautiful women were waiting for us to accompany them. Tom, meet Dorothy Banks and Ginny Speares."

"Are you sure you'll have enough room?" The gal named Ginny leaned closer. Bill hadn't taken his gaze from her bright blue eyes and mirrored her every move. It was almost comical to watch.

"No problem." Feeling like the odd man out, he led them to his car. He felt like a chauffeur. It wasn't the first time and wouldn't be the last. They crossed the train tracks and pulled into the city park. Tom wove the car along the road until he reached the end of a line of parked cars. Everyone piled out to walk to the pavilion. The sound of a band warming up accompanied the cadence of crickets and cicadas.

Clusters of people congregated around the edges of the open-air pavilion. A few shuffled dance steps along with the music. Tom scanned the crowd, looking for Lainie and her escort. He couldn't shake the bad feeling he had and couldn't understand its source.

❧

Lainie tried to put a little space between her and Lieutenant Daniels. She'd been surprised when he had shown up for dinner and insisted she join him. He'd kept their conversation freewheeling and light. He'd been attentive and made her feel like the center of his world during dinner. When he asked her to accompany him to the dance, she'd gladly tossed aside the current issue of the *Saturday Evening Post* with Norman Rockwell's cover art of Rosie the Riveter.

Now she wondered if she'd been smart to join him.

The band swung into a jive, and Brian kept her on the dance floor. She caught her breath and tried to smile. Maybe she should call a hiatus from dances. A cool breeze tickled the hair away from her neck as they jitterbugged. Dance turned into dance without a pause. Lainie could feel the heat in her cheeks.

"I need a break, Lieutenant."

He eyed her and shook his head. His grip on her tightened, and she fought the urge to squirm. She glanced around, but everyone else seemed absorbed in their companions.

She pushed on his chest. "Let go of me."

"Sir, she's asked you to step back."

Lainie felt a flutter of hope at the sound of that deep, steady voice. A smile touched her lips when Tom Hamilton winked at her over Brian's shoulder. Brian stiffened and turned.

"Soldier, this is no concern of yours."

"She's a friend whose request you've ignored. It is my concern."

Brian pushed Lainie away and whirled on Tom. He punched Tom in the stomach. Lainie stumbled backward and screamed. The music wailed to a halt, and everyone's attention descended on the two soldiers. When the lieutenant noticed, he took a step back and straightened his coat. "Your superior officer will hear about this."

Sid and Bill hurried up and helped Tom to his feet as Brian stalked away.

Lainie scurried up to Tom and clutched his hand. "Are you okay?"

Tom rubbed his stomach and nodded. "Don't think I'll

dance much tonight, though."

"We have to quit meeting like this, or I'll add 'hero' to your list of titles."

Tom laughed and then winced. "I'm far from a hero."

"I hope you don't get in trouble."

They walked away from the crowd and wandered through the park together.

"If I do, it's all right. I have a low tolerance for men who don't listen to their dates."

Heat climbed Lainie's cheeks. "He asked me to join him tonight, and it sounded like fun. Maybe I'll avoid future dances."

"And spend all your nights holed up at Mrs. Babcock's? I doubt that."

"Okay, so that's not a great option. Especially considering me."

"Hmm?"

She stopped and waited until he turned to look at her with a quirked eyebrow. "You really care about the answer, don't you?"

"Yes." He shrugged as if that answer covered everything.

"You are one of a kind, Tom."

He grinned. "What's that make? Five labels? I'm waiting for Superman to join the mix."

"Keep this up, and it might."

Soft conversation filled the space between them as they walked. They crossed the tracks and headed back into Crawford.

Tom pointed to his right. "See that road? The fort extends all the way to this street. I doubt I'll ever explore all of it."

"It seems so contained when you're there."

"You haven't looked for the horses or seen the pack mules." Tom spread his hands wide. "The sheer size of Robinson is why many of us have jobs. Few places could handle thousands of horses and mules at a time. It even makes it the perfect place for dogs, with a ready food supply and room for maneuvers."

Lainie crinkled her nose at the thought. "You don't mean horse meat. . . ."

He nodded. "The dogs have to be fed something, and army surplus works fine."

She shuddered at the thought.

❧

The shops along Main Street had closed, and he steered her around the bars. Tom listened to Lainie talk about her family and friends in North Platte. She quieted, and he realized he'd enjoyed her stories. The people had come to life as she mimicked voices and mannerisms.

"You have a flair for storytelling."

"Is that your way of saying I'm dramatic?" She made a funny face and wrapped her arms around her middle. "Too bad I can't parlay that into something useful."

"How about visiting soldiers at the hospital? I'm sure they'd love the break."

"Maybe someday. Right now it hurts too much. The doctors said I need to be careful for a while."

"Careful about what?"

"I contracted rheumatic fever while in Kentucky. That's why I got sent home." Her shoulders drooped, and she kicked a pebble.

Tom stopped in the well of light from a home's front porch. Shadows had doused the usual sparks in her eyes. "You'll get through this, Lainie."

"Maybe. Not everybody does." She shrugged and walked ahead. "It's my road to walk. Fortunately, most days are good. Unless I overdo it." She looked back at him and smiled. "I'd never do that."

He chuckled. He could see her doing just that.

twelve

May 31, 1943

"So you'll help tonight?" Esther looked at her, palms up in a pleading gesture.

It was only Monday morning, and Lainie already felt overwhelmed. But it wasn't Esther's fault she needed the help enough to beg. "I'll come straight back from work."

When Lainie arrived at the office, Mary was sitting at her desk, looking wan but determined to get back to work. "Sitting at home alone doesn't help."

"I'm glad you're here. You'll never believe what happened while you were gone." Lainie soon had Mary doubled over with laughter as she told stories about Lieutenant Daniels. "So if you run into him, be careful. You now know the story behind the handsome face."

"No need to worry about me." The smile evaporated from Mary's face. "It'll be awhile before I'm ready to enter that world. I'll live vicariously for now."

The day flew in the rough routine Lainie had developed but went more smoothly with Mary and the other girls back.

That night, Lainie rushed to her room to change from her work outfit into a playsuit and skirt. She looked in the mirror and nodded. She could move freely while serving the guests downstairs for dinner. Esther served only two meals: breakfast to her boarders and supper for anyone who came with a dollar and an appetite. Each evening, the dining room filled with a mix of soldiers and townspeople.

Lainie entered the kitchen and slipped on an apron. The scent of chicken and dumplings flavored the room. "Where do you need me?"

Esther looked up from the stove, strands of gray hair pulling out of her bun. "Fill those glasses with water and give one to whoever needs one. Tanya should know who needs to place an order."

Lainie complied and slipped from table to table, depositing glasses on the tables. Tanya focused on the table in front of her as she took an order. Esther offered only a couple of options a night. That kept the menu changing but serving simple. Lainie hadn't heard any complaints about the lack of choices. Instead, the delicious food disappeared, often chased by a slice of pie topped with fresh whipped cream. It smelled like peach pie tonight.

Many of the people in the room looked familiar to Lainie as she worked her way back and forth with food and drinks. That thought pleased her more than she'd expected.

"Hey, sweetheart." A soldier grabbed Lainie's arm as she walked by. "Can you join us for a moment?"

The dining room had emptied as folks finished their meals. Tanya could handle any new people who came in, likely only for dessert. Lainie smiled at the eager private and his companions. "Sure."

One soldier whipped a deck of cards from the stack of games in the corner, and soon they were engaged in a hot game of euchre. Tanya wandered by wiping tables, and Lainie realized she'd never seen the girl interact with anyone beyond the required basics.

"Tanya, come join us. That fella needs someone to make sure he isn't cheating."

"I'd never do that," the private protested.

"Then you count cards."

"Nothing wrong with that." But he sidled his chair over to make room for Tanya. Another guy, this one a sailor, hopped up to pull a chair over.

"So what brings a sailor to an army post?"

"Here to train with dogs. I'm working with four right now, but one isn't working out."

Carefully Lainie pulled Tanya out of her shell and grinned as the girl began to enjoy the game. After they finally kicked the group out, Tanya headed up the stairs but stopped and looked at Lainie. "Thanks."

"The group and game were more fun after you joined us."

Tanya nodded and ran her hand along the banister. "Still, I'm grateful. Good night."

" 'Night." Lainie watched Tanya disappear; then she swept the room with one more gaze. Everything seemed in place for breakfast. She turned out the lights and headed down the hallway toward the small sitting room. A floor-to-ceiling bookshelf lined one wall. Books were stacked and shoved on it with reckless abandon. Her finger ran along the spines, looking for something interesting. She itched to pull all the books off the shelf and instill some order to the chaos.

Many of the books were classics; Dickens, Twain, Austen, Hardy, and more lined several shelves. Then she hit the row of Nebraska authors: Willa Cather, Bess Streeter Aldrich, John Neihardt. She stilled when she reached *A Lantern in Her Hand*. It had been years since she'd read the novel. Was it as good as she remembered? She pulled the book from the shelf and moved across the room to the small settee. Its upholstery had softened with age, and Lainie curled up in the corner.

In no time, she was swept into Abbie Deal's story. Lainie's difficulties faded in importance against the backdrop of survival.

The light flicked off, and Lainie looked up. "Hello?"

"You still up, child?" The light flickered back on, and Esther appeared in the doorway. "I thought you'd turned in."

Lainie lifted the book. "I'm reacquainting myself with an old friend. I hadn't thought of this book since high school."

"It's a good one. Well, I'm off to bed. Morning comes too soon."

Lainie uncurled and stood. "I'll follow you."

"Thanks for helping tonight."

"I didn't do much."

"So you say. I watched you pull Tanya into your group. That was kind. See you in the morning."

❧

Tuesday melted into Wednesday, and Lainie decided to stroll around the parade grounds over lunch. The sun kissed her face, and its warmth felt wonderful. She sat on one of the benches and pulled the book from her bag. She'd just gotten engrossed in the story when she heard her name. She hesitated, hoping it wasn't Lieutenant Daniels, before scanning to see who called. A sailor ran across the parade grounds toward her.

"Hello, Lainie."

She studied him, trying to place him. "Oh, you ate at Mrs. Babcock's earlier this week, didn't you?"

His grin just about split his face in two. "I knew you'd remember, though the guys ribbed me about it."

"Of course I do, but you'll have to help me with your name."

"Seaman Mike Harris, ma'am." He stood taller, and Lainie waited for him to snap a salute.

"At ease." She asked him about his week, and soon he sat next to her, hands flying, as he told her all about his home in New Jersey and what he missed about it. She glanced at her watch and startled. "Sorry, Mike, but I have to get back to work."

He jumped to his feet. "I'll be late, too. It's great to talk to someone." He took a step away before stopping. "Lainie, would you join me at the USO this week? It's a lot to ask. . . ."

"I'd decided to take a break from that for a while." His face fell, and Lainie wondered what harm would really come of it. Surely the incident with the lieutenant was an anomaly. Most men prior to him had treated her with respect. Then the image of Tom in a red Superman cape came to mind, and she fought a giggle. Maybe Tom would wait on standby. "I can make an exception, since you're only in town a few more weeks."

"Wonderful! I'll come by the office tomorrow or Friday." He hurried off.

As she watched him go, she realized she wasn't in North Platte anymore. These boys weren't stopping for a twenty-minute break while their trains refueled. She'd need to be more careful. Fortunately, Mike seemed like a nice boy, but she'd thought the same of Brian Daniels.

❧

Private Bill Byers flipped over the shoulder of the martial arts instructor, who'd arrived from Denver. Tom watched the action from the intermittent shade of a ponderosa pine. He'd slid as far from the action as he could without calling attention to himself. The moves the instructor demonstrated looked painful. He'd be grateful for learning them if he ever saw combat. Knowing his luck, he'd look more the fool than Bill had. The instructor called for his next victim, and John Tyler clambered to his feet.

"Now, Private, I want you to rush at me." The instructor turned toward the assembled men. "Notice my feet are spread shoulder-width apart, knees slightly bent. This puts me in a better position to redirect his energy as he comes at me." The man beckoned as if coaxing a reluctant dog toward him.

John cocked his head and eyed the ground behind the man. It was clear of rocks and other obstacles, but Tom thought it looked like a mighty hard landing spot. John rolled his shoulders then lowered his center of gravity by crouching forward. With a war whoop, he rushed the instructor, who casually sidestepped and let John fly by him.

"Much of hand-to-hand combat is keeping your opponent off balance and using your body as a lever with which you'll toss theirs where you will."

John rolled to a sitting position with a wild look in his eye. "Can I try again?"

"Ready when you are." The instructor resumed his odd bent-leg stance.

John rushed the instructor but this time used his leg to

sweep the instructor's legs out from under him. He looked down at the instructor where he sprawled in the prairie grass. "Another rule is to make your opponent underestimate you."

The instructor chuckled and reached up a hand. John hauled him to his feet, and he brushed off his seat. "Duly noted, Private, but that would only work if you got a second chance. Unlikely in combat. Next victim, please."

After watching several more, Tom stood for his turn. He eyed the instructor and tried to think of some strategy that wouldn't land him on his back. Most of the others had stared at the sky and shaken their heads as they stood. The trick seemed to be feinting to one side or the other to knock the instructor off balance. Pulling in a lungful of air, Tom zigzagged toward the man. Just as he thought it might work, he felt a hand or foot connect with his hips, and he cartwheeled through the air. He landed with an *oohf* and screwed his eyes shut against the sun's glare. Something tickled his neck, and he slapped it away.

"Want another shot?" The instructor stood over him and offered him a hand up.

Tom accepted the help and shook each arm and leg, relieved they seemed intact.

"Rush me from behind." The instructor looked at the group. "When someone is coming from behind, you'll need to lean forward, almost roll, as they connect with you. That will propel them over the top."

Tom waited as the instructor turned to face the others. Tom rushed forward and tried to wrap the instructor in a bear hug. They tumbled to the ground, and the instructor sprang up with a grin. "That's how it's done, men. In war, you only have one shot to get this right."

Those words rang in Tom's head as he walked back to the barracks. So much of life was about getting things right the first time. He hoped he wouldn't fail if his chance came.

thirteen

June 4, 1943

Lainie looked in the mirror and dabbed on some red lipstick. She pulled her strand of pearls out of its box and put them on. The drape of her dress's neckline was the perfect foil for the pearls. And the full, pleated skirt would whirl nicely as she danced at the USO.

Esther stuck her head in the room. "Better stop primping and get downstairs. Your soldier's waiting and nervous as a calf during branding season."

With a last glance in the mirror, Lainie grabbed her pumps. The stocking lotion had done the trick in giving her legs the look of nylons. She twirled and curtsied in front of Esther.

"You're lovely as a model in that dress. That blue highlights your eyes. Go on now."

Lainie smiled and hurried downstairs. Mike stood at the bottom of the stairs, shifting from foot to foot. He clutched a bouquet of wildflowers, squeezing the stems so hard his knuckles were white. The wild indigo and ground plum formed the perfect backdrop for the delicate white lady's slippers.

"Those flowers are beautiful."

"Not as lovely as you." His voice squeaked, and he cleared his throat. "Here."

She accepted the bouquet and buried her nose in it. Fingering the pouchlike slipper on one flower, she marveled at the smooth petal. "These are wonderful. Let me put them in some water."

"Yes, ma'am."

Lainie hurried to the kitchen and filled a glass with water. She shoved the cluster in the glass and returned to the hallway. "I'll leave these here for now. Let's go."

Mike settled her into his car and walked around to the driver's side. He slid in and sat ramrod straight for a minute.

"Are you all right, seaman?"

He swallowed and stared straight ahead. "Missing my girl, ma'am."

"First, quit calling me *ma'am*. I doubt I'm much older than you, so Lainie will do fine. Second, why don't you tell me about her while we drive."

Once he started talking, Lainie wondered if he'd stop. She soon felt as if she'd met this Rebecca Miniver and would know her on sight. "I can tell she means a lot to you."

"I'm sorry to carry on."

"Don't worry. We'll walk into the USO, and you'll have a good time. One that you can tell her all about. Frankly, I'm relieved you have a girl back home. It'll make it easier when you leave if we're only friends."

He turned and studied her in the pale glow of the streetlight that filtered through the windshield. "Thank you."

"Let's dance, sailor."

❧

The wail of a trumpet pierced the room and brought the USO to life. Couples jumped up from their seats and rushed to the floor. The wail turned into an instrumental version of "Boogie Woogie Bugle Boy." Tom stayed in his chair and watched the couples swing into the jitterbug. He rubbed his shoulder and rotated his arm. A nice deep bruise had shown up over the last twenty-four hours, probably a result of one too many flying leaps over shoulders.

The fort's orchestra slowed down its tempo and switched to a decent rendition of Glenn Miller's "In the Mood." Time for refreshments.

He stood and bumped his way around the floor to a table loaded down with cake and cookies and a bowl of punch.

Other beverages were available at the bar in the next room. He smiled at the two young ladies behind the table. The chaperones had brought a busload of women to the dance from Alliance.

A striking redhead handed him a glass of punch. "Enjoy."

He nodded. "Thank you." He turned and bumped into a woman with hair as dark as the night sky.

"Fancy meeting you here." Lainie's eyes sparkled and matched her smile.

"Doesn't look like you need a hero tonight."

She shook her head. "No, the seaman I'm with is over the moon for a girl back home. Exactly the kind I like to spend time with. Though I wouldn't mind talking about something else. At least he can dance."

"Save one or two for me."

She quirked an eyebrow and studied him for a moment. He wondered what she saw. "Make sure you find me."

A broad-shouldered sailor walked up beside her. He placed his hand on the small of Lainie's back as he sized Tom up. "You all right, Lainie?"

"Sure am. Mike, meet my friend Tom Hamilton. Tom, this is Mike Harris."

Tom shook hands with the seaman. "Nice to meet you. I'll be by for that dance, Lainie."

The couple strolled off, and Tom settled back to wait for an appropriate time to collect his dance and leave. Then again, with her track record, maybe he'd stick around. This sailor seemed protective, a marked improvement over that last guy.

He couldn't figure out Lainie Gardner. She enjoyed his company, but from the looks of things, he was far from the only one. The shuffling of a couple hundred feet against the floor stilled as the bandleader announced a break. Lainie whispered something in the seaman's ear and then walked toward Tom. She fanned her face.

"Take me out for fresh air?"

Tom nodded and offered her his arm. Lainie looped her arm through his, and they worked their way outside.

"Lainie, do you have plans tomorrow?"

"No. There aren't an abundance of distractions in Crawford."

"Then join me. I'm going riding. It'll be a beautiful day, one made to spend outside."

She looked at him, concern on her face. "A horse? I've never ridden before."

"No problem. We have some gentle animals in the barns. I can commandeer one for you. Explore the hills around us."

"I'm game." A smile replaced her frown.

"I'll pick you up at ten o'clock."

"Should I pack a picnic?"

Tom nodded, the vision of a day spent out in God's wonderful creation filling him with excitement. "That would be great. We can take it with us. Don't forget some apples or carrots to share with the horses."

"All right."

"Have a great night, Lainie."

He'd returned to the barracks before he realized he'd never collected on his dance.

❧

The next morning Lainie stood in the kitchen watching Esther put together a picnic basket for her. Esther added a container of homemade coleslaw to the basket that overflowed with cold fried chicken, cookies, apples, and a bottle of milk.

"That should do it."

Lainie eyed it and nodded. "I think that's plenty. We'll be gone only a couple hours."

"All that fresh air could make you extra hungry."

"You're assuming we'll find a horse that likes me." Lainie grabbed the basket before Esther could stuff anything else in it. "Thank you."

She took the basket and walked to the front porch, where she sank onto the top step to wait. Several cars moved up and down the street. The sun warmed her face, and the scent of roses filled the air. Tom had been right; this would be the perfect day to spend outside.

Thirty minutes later as she stared at horses that towered over her in the barn, she wanted to retract her agreement. "You seriously want me to climb on the back of one of these beasts?"

"Yes. We'll find a gentle one for you. The WACs love to ride, so Private Thorson here is used to matching women with horses."

Lainie eyed the skinny soldier and wondered what qualified him. "Aren't you a little small for a soldier?"

"I'm a world-class jockey on loan to the army. Edgar Thorson at your service."

"I can see your ego more than makes up for your stature."

"Yes, miss, and this horse is perfect for you."

He led a dappled gray horse toward her. Lainie stepped back to avoid getting trampled. The horse's back easily met her shoulders.

Tom grabbed her hands and forced her to look at him. "Lainie, you can do this. And you'll love it. You love your freedom, and nothing is better than racing across a field on horseback."

Spots floated in her vision, and her breath caught in her chest. Concern flashed across Tom's face. "Don't worry. We won't race today. We'll let the horses walk, maybe canter, but only if you want to."

The horse snorted and lowered its head to nuzzle her shoulder. Lainie took another step back and shook her head. She considered the horse. Would it really feel like freedom to race across the plains on its back? "What's this thing's name?"

Private Thorson grinned at her. "Daisy."

"Exactly the name I would have chosen." The horse pawed the ground and stepped toward her. "Persistent thing, isn't she?" Lainie reached up and ran her fingers along the velvety muzzle. She inhaled a breath that carried the mixed scent of hay, horse, and sunshine. "You'd better get me on her before I change my mind."

Private Thorson led Daisy toward a block of wood standing next to the barn. "All you need to do is hop up on this block. Then grab the saddle horn with both hands. I'll hold her steady while you put your left foot in the stirrup and throw your right leg across her back."

"I'm sure it's that simple." Lainie rolled her eyes and pulled Tom with her as she stalked to the block. "You'd better catch me when she bucks me off."

"Daisy hasn't bucked in a long time, miss. Talk to her softly, and let her know you're getting ready to climb on."

Tom helped Lainie onto the block. Once perched on it, she drew in a shaky breath and tried to still her shaking hands. Sure, she'd loved *Black Beauty* as a child, but this was a first. It should be easier than this, but her hands refused to grab the horn.

fourteen

Daisy flicked an ear at a fly, and a barn cat strutted out of the shadows to watch. Tom rubbed a hand over his chin to wipe the smile off his face that wanted to sneak out. If Lainie caught him laughing at her, he could imagine her reaction. Lots of sparks.

"Come on, Lainie. Daisy's a patient lady, but every horse has her limits." Daisy snorted and pawed the ground at Tom's words.

Private Thorson turned on the charm. "Both hands on the saddle horn. There. Now stick your left foot in the stirrup. Not that left foot. There you go. Now up and over. Good." He winked at Tom. "Hold Daisy while I grab Tornado."

Lainie perched on top of the saddle, back stiff and chin high. Tom shielded his eyes from the sun to get a better look. Yep, a blank expression tightened the muscles around her eyes, and she looked ready to swoon. "We can do something else if you'd rather."

"No." The word sliced the air. "We'll do this, but if I get hurt, so help me, Tom."

"I won't let anything happen to you." He would do everything in his power to protect her from harm. Maybe someday she'd understand how serious he was.

Thorson brought out a gelding that stamped his feet in impatience. The horse tossed his head, mane flying. "Hey, boy. Good to see you, too."

"You act like good friends."

"I try to ride him as often as I can. Tornado and I enjoy a good run, don't we?" The horse pawed the ground with his right foreleg. "Thanks, Thorson. We'll be back in a few hours."

"Don't forget this." Thorson tossed the repacked picnic to him, and Tom pulled the knapsack over his shoulders. "Have a good time. And relax, miss; Daisy'll take care of you."

Lainie pulled her hat lower over her eyes and nodded. "Thank you." She turned her head with a stiff jerk toward Tom. "How do I get her to move?"

"Squeeze her lightly with your knees. She'll get the idea." Tom on Tornado led Lainie and Daisy up the road and away from the highway. They clopped past the parade grounds and struck out from the post buildings. Within minutes, the barracks and officers' quarters were behind them, the sandy hills and buttes in front of them. Peace descended on Tom as it so often did when he sneaked away for some time in God's creation. Some might call it rugged, but he thought the area showcased God's diversity and creativity.

"How ya doing, Lainie?"

Her body swayed in time with Daisy's gait. She remained perfectly balanced even as she gripped the reins so tightly her knuckles were white.

"I'm okay, though I'm not sure I can climb off her."

"I'll help." A funny feeling flooded his stomach at the thought of lifting Lainie from the horse. She'd been light in his arms when dancing. And he could only imagine how she'd feel as he handed her down. He swallowed and forced the sensation away. They had only friendship, and that was as it should be.

They traveled in silence. When she'd been quiet awhile, he glanced over to see if she'd fallen asleep. He'd seen it happen to others lulled by the gentle pacing of a horse's walk. She caught his glance and gamely tried to smile.

"I think I'm getting the hang of this."

"You look like a natural."

"Sure I do." Her shoulders dropped a bit, and the reins came to rest lightly in her hands and across the saddle. "Thank you for talking me into this."

"My pleasure." A copse of chokecherry shrubs appeared a

hundred yards in front of them. They were covered in yellow blossoms and would provide some shade. A thin rivulet ran behind the grove. "Let's head there for lunch. The horses can drink and forage while we eat."

He ground-hobbled the horses and reached up to help Lainie off Daisy. She grasped his hands tightly and swung her right leg over the horse. She groaned and slid into his arms. His heart raced as his breath stilled. Her head fit perfectly under his chin, and she sagged into him.

"I'm not sure my legs will support me. It feels like I'm still moving." She murmured the words against his chest.

"Give yourself a moment." He knew he should step back, put some space between them, but she leaned on him. How could he do it without dropping her on the ground? She looked up, a grimace marring her delicate features.

"Remind me to think twice next time. Parts of my legs ache I didn't know could hurt."

"It'll get better." He stepped back and pulled her toward the shade. "Let's enjoy that lunch you brought."

Lainie uncurled as they ate. Her sharp wit kept him on his toes, and he liked that feeling. He didn't have to wonder what she thought. She'd tell him without hesitation. They cleaned up the traces of the picnic, and he boosted her onto Daisy. A crease furrowed her brow, and she looked from him to the countryside.

"Even if I'm sore, thanks for encouraging me to come. It's amazing out here." Daisy flicked an ear toward her. Lainie smiled and leaned forward to rub Daisy's neck. "And you have lived up to your billing. Not bad for a first ride."

"I knew you'd like this." Tom hopped on Tornado and pulled the animal's head toward the fort. "Anytime you want to go out again, let me know. I'll take any excuse to break away and experience the peace out here."

❧

Esther pounded on the door Sunday morning. "Time to get moving or you'll miss church."

Lainie cracked open her eyes and squinted against the glare of sunshine streaming into the room. She shifted her legs to the side of the bed and bit off a squeal. Shards of heat skittered through her thighs, and her shoulders balled tight. She groaned and focused on releasing each group of muscles.

"Are you awake in there?" An echo of concern filled Esther's voice.

"I'll be down in a minute." Lainie gritted her teeth and pushed up. This was the pain of muscles used, not of muscles abused by fever. She should feel grateful. Instead, she wanted to question her sanity. Then she thought of the freedom she'd felt abandoning the fort and roaming the hills with Tom. Everything from the delicate chokecherry flowers to the scraggly branches of pines stretching toward heaven had hinted at the handiwork of God. Only He could make everything so unique and detailed. If He cared so much about the details of creation, why couldn't He care as intimately about her?

It must be Sunday if such thoughts rolled through her mind. The answers danced beyond her reach, so she forced the questions away. Maybe someday she'd find an answer that made sense when compared to the reality of her life.

"If I don't hear some movement, I'm coming in." The door handle rattled in its catch.

"All right." Lainie stood up with a thud. "Did you hear that, Esther? I'm moving."

"Good thing. We've got to hustle, missy." The sound of Esther thumping down the hallway and muttering to herself filtered through the door.

Lainie shook her head and wondered if she'd have to hobble to church. "You'd think the horses would be the sore ones."

ॐ

All week, Lainie looked for Tom but never saw him closer than across a field. If she didn't know better, she'd think he was purposefully avoiding her. He almost turned on his heel if they came within one hundred yards of each other.

He'd seemed to enjoy Saturday, and the conversation had flowed back and forth with plenty of barbs. As she sat at her desk Wednesday, she could almost feel the heat of the sun warming her face. Surely he'd enjoyed it as much as she. But the more she analyzed their time, the more she worried that she'd done or said something wrong. For the life of her, she couldn't figure out what that was, but he'd turned inward the closer they came to the fort.

Instead, she kept running into Lieutenant Daniels. The heat in his eyes made it clear he continued to fume. At least he glowered from a distance.

That afternoon, Mary stopped in front of Lainie's desk. "You're a million miles away today. Something wrong?"

Lainie shook her head and turned back to the intake papers piled on the desk. "Gathering wool, I guess."

"Are there many Gardners in North Platte?"

"No, all of Father's family is from Kansas. His job at the bank brought our family to town. Why?"

"I wondered because Private Donahue brought in the newest stack of forms. This top one says the dog belonged to James Gardner of North Platte."

Lainie bolted out of the chair and rushed around the table. "Let me see that." She scanned the sheet once then again, unwilling to believe the information typed on the page. "No, no, no. Why would they do that?" She spun and grabbed her hat from the coat tree before rushing from the building.

She stepped into the sunlight and stopped. Where could she go? She couldn't let the army have Mason. The dog had been her confidant on too many occasions to count. The black Lab would settle back on her haunches and listen as Lainie poured out her woes. Mason didn't have an aggressive bone in her body and didn't chase every squirrel and bird like so many of her breed. "What were they thinking?" Mason would flop as a war dog, although part of Lainie feared the dog would excel with her intelligence. Lainie had to find her and get Mason discharged before the training harmed her.

But what could she do? Her thoughts froze in a jumbled mess, and she felt rooted to the ground. Lainie shook her head and forced herself forward. Maybe Mason was still in processing. If so, she'd be at the war dog reception center. Lainie hurried across the street to the center.

She pushed open the doors and waited for her eyes to adjust to the dimness. The smell of antiseptic and bleach mixed with doggy odor choked her. She covered her mouth and nose and looked for anyone who might be in charge. Her gaze fixed on Sergeant Lewis. He could help her—he had to.

"Sergeant." She rushed toward him when he didn't move. "Sergeant, please, I need to talk to you for a moment."

He turned from the dog he'd been examining and looked at her. "Yes, Miss Gardner? What can I do for you?"

"Please, there's been a mistake." She thrust the papers at him. "This dog, she shouldn't be here."

"And how do you know that?"

"She's my family pet."

"Not anymore. Says right there she's property of the War Department for the duration."

Lainie's knees weakened, and she closed her eyes. She felt someone grab her arm. Clenching her teeth, she yanked her arm free. "I want her back. If my family's decided they no longer want her, I'll take her."

"Can't do that."

She opened her eyes and blinked away the tears clouding her vision. "She doesn't have the personality to be a war dog."

"If that's true, we'll find out during the training exercises." He shrugged. "The dog's in the army now. I suggest you accept that."

Lainie spun to leave before the tears fell down her cheeks. The sergeant might think there was nothing she could do about Mason. Lainie refused to accept that. She'd find a way. She had to.

fifteen

June 10, 1943

Lainie waltzed into the K-9 office, a smile plastered on her lips. In her hands, she carried a still-warm strawberry-rhubarb pie. Sarge had been at Mrs. Babcock's earlier that week, enjoying a slice. Maybe he'd enjoy this one enough to see things her way.

She couldn't wait until the military realized they'd made a terrible mistake in accepting Mason.

"Good morning, Sarge."

"Miss Gardner." The man licked his lips as he eyed her package. Lainie perked up. Maybe this would work.

"That smells mighty good."

"One of Mrs. Babcock's special pies."

"Now why would you bring that to me? It wouldn't have anything to do with that dog of yours?"

Lainie bit her lower lip. She must proceed carefully, get him to at least listen to her. "Does a girl need a reason to bring a gift?"

"Usually, yes. Why don't you tell me what it is you want?"

"Mason." The word exploded from her mouth. She pasted her lips together and took a breath. "Did you have a dog growing up?"

"Sure. Most kids do."

"Mason is that dog for me. I may have been a senior in high school, but she's been a special friend. I can't just accept that she's in the army. It's not what she's supposed to do." Lainie placed the box on top of Sarge's battered desk.

He pulled the box to him and lifted the lid. "Smells like strawberry-rhubarb. Nobody makes it like Mrs. Babcock."

"I know." She slumped as she read the set of his shoulders.

"You won't help me, will you?"

"Look, Miss Gardner. Much as I like you and appreciate the pie, the army has regulations that cannot be violated. Not for anybody. And not as a result of any bribe. You may not believe this, but I do understand." He pushed the pie back to her. "Bribe or no, Mason stays unless she shows she's unfit for duty."

A tear trickled down Lainie's cheek, and she brushed it away. Spinning on her heel, she hurried toward the door. "Keep the pie."

As she headed back to her office, Lainie wanted to cover her ears to hide the sound of the dogs. Their barking seemed especially loud this morning. The sound hammered home how much she had failed Mason.

❧

Lainie stalked across the grass leading toward the dog pens. Her dark curls bounced against her shoulders, and fire sparked from her eyes. Tom stilled and considered ducking behind the truck in front of him. What crazy idea did she harbor this time? Since Mason had arrived at the center a week ago, Lainie had gone mad. Every day, she had a new scheme to free her dog from the army. She refused to accept that the army didn't work that way.

Last night, she'd cornered him.

"Tom, you have to help me." She turned her face into a pleading mask. "No one else will listen."

Her spine had stiffened, and she'd spit fire when he told her he couldn't help. The army had rules, and he lived within them. He'd expected the flames to scorch his back as she left. Tom didn't want to experience a fresh wave of her anger.

She hesitated when her gaze landed on him. Then she squared her shoulders and glared past him as if he'd disappeared. Nope, she hadn't forgotten.

The set to her chin raised a red flag in his gut. He didn't know what she'd decided, but she'd made some decision. Tom followed her from a safe distance. Whatever she was up to, she might need help. Or someone to prevent her from doing something careless.

She stalked over the hill. He'd hoped she'd turn left toward the obstacle course or the water source. Instead, she aimed straight for the kennels. His heart started to pound to the beat of reveille. Hadn't she learned anything while she worked here? Just last week, another soldier had landed in the infirmary with serious bites. How did she think she'd fare if an animal responded to her presence with aggression? If a large, square-shouldered soldier had lost the fight, a slip of a girl would experience worse.

Her steps didn't falter until she passed the first row of waist-high trees. Someday they'd shade the dogs. Today they marked the beginning of a new section of dogs. Six rows down, she turned to walk down the aisle.

"Lainie, stop." He tried to infuse his voice with command, but she continued on. "Lord, why is she so stubborn?"

He held his breath. She'd miscalculated as she counted. Mason's crate stood one section over. Tom didn't know these animals well, and he examined their reactions to the invader. Some merely lay beside their kennels and watched. Others stood at attention and barked aggressively. A couple, though, had a look in their eyes that pushed Tom to close the gap between them.

"Lainie, stop now." He bellowed the words, a vise gripping his chest.

She jolted to a stop and turned on him. "Who do you think you are? Yesterday you wouldn't help. And now you'll tell me what to do? Who gave you the right?"

"Look at the dogs."

She jerked her head from side to side. "What? There are a thousand dogs here, but I only care about one."

"But you should care about all of them. These dogs are training to become attack dogs. Didn't you read *Hoofbeats and Barks*? See the article about the attack? That could be you." He stared at her and tried to slow the rush of words, fight the tightening in his chest. "Come to me now. Let's get you out of here and then discuss this."

She snorted. "These are dogs, Tom. They aren't going to hurt me."

"No, these are war machines, most trained to attack intruders. Take a look around. You're invading their territory."

A movement to the left caught Tom's attention. He turned and saw a German shepherd pulling against its chain.

"Lainie, come to me now."

She followed his gaze and finally moved toward him. The dog lunged as she darted past. She screamed and leapt to the side. "Tom, help me."

He gulped against the fear and raced toward her, placing his body between her and the German shepherd. "Run." He watched her dart back to safety, trying to keep an eye fixed on the dog. The dog lunged, and hot breath and snapping teeth dug at Tom's arm. He shook his arm from the dog's reach and raced away. When he reached Lainie, he doubled over and drew a shuddering breath.

"That is why you cannot come here. Lainie, you'll lose. Every time."

She grabbed at his sleeve, turning it over and twisting the fabric, probing for tears.

"Are you all right? I am so sorry." The words rushed past her lips, her voice higher than usual, her eyes wide and dilated. "I could have been attacked. And you're hurt."

He placed his hands on each side of her face and forced her gaze from his arm to him. "I'm okay. It's a scratch. See, hardly any blood."

She shook her head and focused on him. "Are you sure?"

"Yes. Promise you'll never do anything that stupid again."

Lainie nodded, and a tear slipped from one eye. He lightly brushed it away and traced its trail. Her breath hitched, and she shivered. His stomach tightened at the smoothness of her skin. He backed away, dropping his arms to his side. "These aren't family pets. You have to remember that."

"That's why I have to get Mason back. She'll be destroyed in this process. She's not an aggressive dog." She wrapped her arms around her middle. "I can't let that happen."

The urge to shelter her in an embrace, protect her from her fear, overwhelmed him. As he debated what to do, Lainie turned away and slipped over the hill.

❧

On Thursday, Tom still stewed about Lainie's actions and abrupt departure. Thoughts of her generated a war. Part of him wanted to find and comfort her; the other, to shake her until she understood how dangerous and foolish her actions were. And every time he thought they might form a friendship that went beyond saving Lainie from herself, she acted without thinking.

Tom shook his head and tried to pull his thoughts from the raven beauty with bad decision-making skills and back to the obstacle course he faced.

Sarge Allen stood in front of the basic trainees, hands on hips, feet spread apart in a balanced stance. "This afternoon your task is to complete this course."

Groans rose from behind Tom, but he refused to turn. The pack sat heavy on his shoulders. It shifted from side to side with each step regardless of how he secured it. And his boots chafed his feet, reopening blisters. Whoever had decided boots were a good idea for long hikes and runs hadn't tried it.

"You have two hours to complete the course. You will be judged on how quickly you complete it. The sooner you're back here, the quicker we can head to the firing range." The private next to Tom moaned, and Tom jutted out his jaw, waiting for the attack. Sarge skewered him with a look but held his tongue. He pulled the stopwatch out of his pocket and clicked the timer. "Go."

The men quickly closed ranks and jogged down the path. They'd run as a pack for the first quarter of the rugged course. Then the hills and rocks would take their toll on the heavier men.

The ranks started to thin, but Tom kept his thoughts focused on the end. "I can do everything through Him who gives me strength." The verse pounded through his head in cadence to the beat of his feet on the hard-packed earth.

Sid jogged up next to him, breathing regularly with barely a drop of sweat on his forehead. "Hanging in there?"

Tom growled as rivers of sweat poured between his shoulder blades and the pack.

"That good? Think of our Class A passes waiting for this weekend."

"I might not still be alive."

"Yeah, you will. You'll do this if I have to drag your sorry carcass through the course."

Tom ground his teeth and grimaced. "With friends like you. . ."

"You don't have to thank me."

"Great. Go encourage someone else."

Sid turned around and ran backward a few steps. "Aren't we testy?"

"Show-off." Tom caught the rest of what he wanted to say. What had happened to his earlier attitude? Paul hadn't meant he could do all things through Christ including taking off a buddy's head with his words. "Sorry, Sid. I'm glad we're over halfway. This schedule is brutal."

"Just think, the guns are next. You're stealing the show with those."

Two hours later, his sweaty cheek pressed into his rifle's butt, Tom hadn't hit a thing. At this rate, he wouldn't hit the broadside of a barn back at the fort.

They were hunkered down for crawl drills. He inhaled a slow stream of air and steadied his cheek against the rifle's butt. Dirt covered his uniform, and the pack pressed him farther into the sand. The grit had found its way between his teeth and between his toes. Tom tried to force his mind past the discomfort to a zone that focused on the target one hundred paces ahead. He knew how to do this. Years of hunting everything that moved in Wyoming had made him skilled with a rifle. Until people started scoring his shots, that was.

Almost half the guys in the first session qualified for marksmanship badges. He could do no less. Not in the one military skill he usually excelled at.

Tom blew out the breath and eased another one in. He sighted down the barrel of the gun and squeezed the trigger. The M1 Garand recoiled against his cheek. There, that felt the way it should. Straight and true. He sighted down the barrel again and saw a hole in the target's chest. He squeezed off seven more rounds, emptying the clip. Each felt more natural than the one before it.

"Woo-hee. Look who's found his target." Sergeant Huber stopped and hunkered down next to Tom. "I'd begun to worry about you, but looks like that was misplaced."

"Yes, sir." Tom pushed himself up on his elbows, ready to insert another clip.

"All right, men. That's enough for today. If you all progress like Specialist Hamilton, we may win this war."

Sid war-whooped, and Tom looked for a boulder to hide behind. Attention was the last thing he needed. He licked his teeth and grimaced at the grit. No, all he wanted was a shower and a slice of Mrs. Babcock's pie. On second thought, that appealed only if Lainie joined him.

sixteen

June 18, 1943

The sun sailed above the horizon even though it was after five o'clock.

" 'Night, Lainie. Have a good weekend."

"You, too, Mary." Lainie looked around the empty office and sagged into her chair. Another week's work finished, yet the last place she wanted to go was home. She could always stay and head over to the officers' club or USO, but neither appealed to her. No matter how she tried, she couldn't shake the funk she'd fallen into when she realized she could do nothing to free Mason. Isolation overwhelmed her when everybody—even Tom—refused to help.

Lainie searched the sky and weighed her options. Maybe she could take Daisy for a ride. She might not be the world's best horsewoman, but a couple of quick rides during lunch had increased her comfort in the saddle.

Gray clouds painted a blaze across the horizon. If she hurried, she'd have time for a short ride. She pulled her bag from beneath her desk and changed into the pair of pants she'd brought with her. When she reached the barn, Private Thorson was mucking out a stall.

"You're still here." Lainie smiled down at the man. "Would you mind terribly saddling Daisy for me?"

He looked out the window at the sky then at her. "Only if you'll stay close. Storms can flare up quickly."

"I promise." A rush of energy surged through Lainie at the thought of the wind blowing through her curls. She needed a taste of freedom. Then she could refocus on life and its disappointments.

Private Thorson threw the rake to the side and whistled. Several horses perked up, but only Daisy trotted toward him. Her black tail fanned behind her like a flag, and her ears twitched to the front as if she waited for instructions. In minutes, Private Thorson bounced Lainie into the saddle. "Remember to stick close to the parade grounds."

Lainie nodded and turned Daisy's head toward the road. They clipped to the end of the officers' quarters, and Daisy continued past more stables. Lainie let Daisy pick the path and focused on the stark beauty of the land. Tom had led her in this general direction, and she trusted Daisy.

Daddy had called last night. Lainie couldn't shake how certain he'd sounded. She'd tried to tell him her concerns about Mason and how hurt she'd been when she learned he'd sent Mason to Dogs for Defense.

"Get over it, girlie. You're doing your part, and Mason will do hers." His voice had sounded hard, indifferent.

A chill shook Lainie, and she rubbed her arms. She examined the terrain and realized that while she'd been lost in thought, Daisy had carried her past the fort toward the hills. Daisy picked her way up a rise, and Lainie grabbed for the saddle horn. She tried to time her movements to match the horse's but couldn't find the rhythm. Daisy's foot caught a dip in the ground, and she stumbled. Lainie grabbed her mane and hung on.

"Easy, girl."

The wind picked up and whistled through the pine trees. Lainie's skin pebbled. The sun hid behind a bank of clouds, and the temperature dipped. Lainie eyed the sky, and her stomach tightened at the angry clouds.

"We'd better turn around, Daisy." She pulled against the reins and waited for Daisy to comply. Before they'd traveled one hundred feet down the butte, raindrops pelted her skin in an angry staccato. Lainie pushed soaked curls out of her face. "Find shelter, girl."

Lightning flashed, followed within seconds by thunder.

Daisy forgot her gentle nature and reared. Lainie screamed and fought to stay on her back. The horse danced, trying to keep her feet. When more lighting zigzagged across the sky, Daisy bolted across the plain. Lainie kept her hold on the saddle horn and clung to a handful of mane. Her legs gripped the flanks, and she tucked her head against Daisy's neck. She didn't know where they were and couldn't see through the rain.

Fear gripped Lainie. Her hair was plastered to her face, and she fought against panic for each breath. Daisy had to find the stable and soon. As the deluge continued, Lainie struggled to maintain her grip as shivers racked her frame.

❧

"You have to let me go after her." Tom pushed past Edgar Thorson and grabbed Tornado's halter.

Thorson crossed his arms and planted himself in front of Tom. "You can't do that. This storm makes it dangerous for anyone in it."

"Especially a woman who hardly knows how to ride. That's why I have to go after her."

"Hold on there, Private." Sarge Lewis hurried into the stables. "She's one of my girls, but we can't go after her until the storm blows over. Soon as it does, we'll send dog teams out. They'll find her in no time."

Tom ground his teeth to stop the flow of words. Didn't they understand? She didn't know what she was doing. What had she been thinking to disappear with a storm coming in? He wanted to find her, and then Tom couldn't decide if he would shake her or kiss her. She had no business putting herself in this kind of danger.

"I'll get a couple of the teams on standby." Sarge pulled the hood of his rain slicker over his head and dashed out into the downpour.

"She doesn't know this area." Tom walked to the doorway and tried to make out anything through the dark storm.

Thorson stepped next to him. "But Daisy does. She knows

where her food and shelter are. She'll bring Miss Gardner back."

Tom searched the darkness for Lainie and hoped Thorson was right. An hour later, Tom's stomach growled, but he refused to abandon his post. The rain eased up, and Tom hoped the gathered teams would move out soon. If they couldn't, he thought he'd go crazy with worry.

One of the dogs, a Lab, jumped to attention. His handler brushed his fur, encouraging him to relax, but the animal didn't budge. "Looks like Rocket has something."

Tom scanned the darkness, gut twisting with the need to see.

Other soldiers hurried to the door and joined him.

"I think I hear something."

Thorson perked up. "That's got to be Daisy."

Tom stepped into the night, unable to hear anything above the rain. But as he searched the darkness, he saw a wall of black moving toward him. On its back, a flash of white. Lainie.

Thorson raced past him and grabbed Daisy's reins. "Tom, get her off the horse."

Tom rubbed Lainie's hand. It felt ice cold. She hadn't dressed to get caught in a storm. "Lainie, honey, can you hear me?"

She stirred and moaned.

"I'm going to slide you off Daisy, okay?"

She barely nodded and leaned toward him. He caught her effortlessly, and another soldier wrapped a blanket around her.

"Take her to the hospital?"

"No. It's full, and she's a civilian. She'll be more comfortable at Mrs. Babcock's." His chest pounded as he stared at her face. She was so still. He whisked her into the cab of a truck Sid had pulled up, cradling her against his chest. Shivers shook her thin frame, and her cheeks were pale as fresh snow.

He pushed his feet against the floorboard, willing the truck to move faster. The heater blasted warm air at them, but the heat didn't seem to reach Lainie. He prayed that somehow

God would protect her, reach through the fog and touch her. Sid whipped the truck in front of Mrs. Babcock's, and Tom lurched forward, unable to brace himself while he held Lainie.

Sid jumped out and ran around to open Tom's door. He unfurled an umbrella and held it over Lainie's face as Tom hurried up the steps. Sid pounded on the door and twisted the knob. They were met by Mrs. Babcock hurrying from the back.

Concern etched fresh lines on her face when she saw Lainie. "What on earth did you do to her? Well, never mind, carry her up the stairs for me. Her room is the second one on the left."

Tom followed Mrs. Babcock as she hurried up the stairs. "Put her on the bed. I'll take care of her from here."

Tom watched helplessly as Mrs. Babcock turned her back on them and bent over Lainie.

"What are you waiting on? Go on. There's nothing you can do now other than pray."

Even as he knew she was right, Tom hated the sinking sensation in his gut.

&

Lainie felt the weight of blankets pressing against her and the soft feather pillow cradling her head. She opened her eyes and squinted against the bright sunlight streaming through the window. Something must be wrong if Esther had let her sleep past breakfast. She shifted. Waves of pain rolled through her.

Daisy must have made her way back to the stable. Vague flashes of memory told Lainie someone had cradled her as if she were a child. She'd had the sensation of being safe. Now she felt pounded by pain and fever.

"She's right through here." The soft murmur of Esther's voice filtered through the door. In a moment, the doorknob twisted, and Esther peeked around the door. "Good. You're awake. Lainie, this is Dr. Gibson."

"Let's take a look at you, young lady." He eased into the chair beside her bed. He looked young, with a minimal sprinkling of gray in his brown hair. Concern radiated from his kind expression. He pulled his bag into his lap and examined her with a look. "Tell me what happened."

Esther slipped from the room, and Lainie told him what she remembered about the storm. "My joints are flaring up again. Could the rheumatic fever be back?" Her heart constricted at the thought of that pain.

He frowned and gently probed her arms and neck. "It's not uncommon for it to flare up during the first several years after the first attack. Did they treat you with penicillin in Kentucky?"

Lainie shook her head. "That was saved for the soldiers."

"Well, I don't have much, but we'll try that. See if we can't get this under control. I haven't tried it myself, but I read a journal article on the treatment. Bed rest for a week, too. Give your body time to fight the fever and let the antibiotic work."

"I don't think so. I've done this before."

"Then you know exactly why you have to obey my orders. Or you'll get sicker. The risk to your heart is greater with each attack."

seventeen

June 20, 1943

The last notes of the closing hymn lingered in the base chapel. The smell of paint touched the air, and sunlight played across the floor in rich colors filtered through the stained glass. The day stretched in front of Tom as he considered his options. After a full Saturday, he had time to relax before another week balancing the demands of basic training and teaching. He'd struggled to focus on his tasks yesterday, but he couldn't shake how cold and wet Lainie had felt. Nor how small she seemed tucked against him.

Had he done enough? Should he have violated orders and chased after her? He thanked God Daisy had found her way back. Mud had covered the horse past her fetlocks, but she'd looked beautiful when she arrived with Lainie on her back.

Tom walked to his car, waving at the guys who yelled but not stopping. A baseball game held no appeal. He had to make sure Lainie was okay. Somehow during the last month, she'd become important to him. He couldn't pinpoint where or how, but he couldn't fight reality. The possibility she didn't feel the same way weighed on his mind. Maybe today he could probe her thoughts.

Puddles dotted the sides of the highway, lingering traces of the storm. He'd found the dogs soaked but otherwise untouched. A few tree limbs dotted the road as he turned into town. He skirted around them, making a mental note to return and clean them up on his return.

The street in front of Mrs. Babcock's was empty. She never opened on Sunday, declaring the Lord's Day too precious to violate. He climbed the steps and knocked on the door.

Minutes passed. He waited. He knocked again, this time louder. Finally, he heard the echo of steps on the wood floor.

A thin girl opened the door and stared at him. She looked all brown with her light brown hair pulled back with a tan ribbon and wearing a dress that matched. He'd seen her before in the dining room, so maybe she boarded here.

"Can I help you?"

"I wondered if I could see Lainie."

The girl stepped back. "Come in, and I'll check with Esther."

Tom did as told, hoping her words weren't as foreboding as they sounded. She showed him to a small parlor that sat to one side. He paced the length of the small room and wondered when Mrs. Babcock would appear.

"Aren't you the picture of a nervous bull?" Mrs. Babcock marched to him. "You can't see her, Tom."

"I promise not to stay. I need to see she's okay."

"The doctor ordered strict bed rest. She's on that new drug, penicillin, too. This isn't the first time she's been sick, and we have to be careful. Doc says her heart could be damaged. According to him, she's lucky that didn't happen the first time."

"Is she okay?"

"She thinks so. She's fighting the bed rest. Pray the drug works and we can keep her down until she's better." Mrs. Babcock shook her head. "The girl's stubborn to the core."

"She wouldn't be here otherwise."

"True. Come back in a couple days." Mrs. Babcock shushed him and stared at the ceiling. "I hear her getting out of bed again. Go before she hears you."

Tom strained to hear whatever Mrs. Babcock had detected. Heaviness cloaked him as a result of her words. Things sounded more serious than he'd anticipated. He'd expected to find Lainie sitting downstairs, reading or playing a game with others. "Should I tell them she won't be at work for a few days?"

"Mary knows." Mrs. Babcock grabbed his arm and walked him to the door. "Good day, Tom."

Before he could say good-bye, he found himself staring at the door. He stood for a moment, hunting for a reason to go back in, but he couldn't. Not if Lainie's health was as fragile as Mrs. Babcock said. As he got into his car, he turned and looked up at the second story. Somewhere, Lainie rested up there. The curtain of the window over the door fluttered, and a hand waved at him to stop. He paused.

The window opened, and Lainie ducked her head out. "Tom, watch Mason till I get back, okay?" Her voice rasped, and he struggled to catch her words.

"Sure, Lainie."

She disappeared from the window, and in a moment it closed. Mrs. Babcock's disapproving figure replaced Lainie's thin frame. Tom started the car and hurried back to base before she could shake another finger at him. He liked her pie too much to get her riled.

That night, he lay on his bunk in the barracks, arms crossed behind his head. The room smelled nothing like the floral air at Mrs. Babcock's. The aroma of too many sweaty boots and men in one place never quite left the air. He'd pop open the window near his bed, but another storm brewed.

Tom stared at the ceiling and tried to imagine a way to help Lainie. Once a family donated a dog through Dogs for Defense, it belonged to the military. If the army no longer needed the dog or if it didn't meet the training requirements, the animal could be returned to the family if they'd requested. He'd examined Mason' paperwork, and Lainie's family wanted nothing more to do with the dog.

Dogs simply weren't returned without a military discharge.

Lainie would never accept that. She must be an only child or baby in the family. She expected the world to bend to her whims.

Only one problem. The army didn't work that way.

૨૭

A million fire ants burrowed into Lainie, and she bit back a scream. She drew in a ragged breath and released it slowly, counting against the pain. She tried to think of an ice cream sundae at Wahl's, an extra cherry decorating the whipped cream. Jumping into the Platte River on a hot day, the cool water splashing her fevered skin. Nothing worked. She was miserable, engulfed by heat burning from the inside out. She bit her lip as her muscles tightened, and a moan slipped from her mouth.

If she called for Esther, the doctor would be back with his negative diagnosis. Lainie would endure this attack. She had to. If Mama and Papa found out how bad things were, they'd have her back home before Lainie could protest.

She couldn't let that happen. Not when she finally had a role, albeit a small one. Her legs jerked beneath the sheet, and a vise tightened around her chest. She struggled to catch a breath and groaned. No question the fever had returned.

The door swung open. Lainie fought to cloak the pain as Dorothy slipped through the door with a glass and a bottle of medicine. "Oh, Lainie." Dorothy hurried to the side of the bed, concern clouding her green eyes. "What can I do to help?"

Lainie shook her head. She felt as if she breathed through a straw.

Dorothy set the cup and bottle on the bedside table. She felt Lainie's forehead, and a frown marred her expression. "You're fever's spiked again. I'm going to get Esther."

Lainie shook her head, but Dorothy had already scooted from the room. So much for convincing Esther she was better.

The sound of a band—probably Tommy Dorsey's—floated up the stairs from the parlor radio. Normally music like that would set her toes tapping and her thoughts swirling. She'd imagine dancing at the USO with a soldier, maybe Tom Hamilton. Not tonight. Tonight even the thought of all he'd done for her couldn't distract her. She tried to imagine his face, his compelling eyes. His image wavered in her mind's eye and then disappeared.

God, help me.

The wardrobe started to dance across the room in time to the beat of the song. She shut her eyes and burrowed into the pillow. She sank into the darkness.

❧

Tom bolted out of bed.

"Where you going, Hamilton?" Billy Brighton rolled over to look at him.

"Checking something out for a friend."

"Keep it down next time you jump like that." Sid shook his head. "You'll have to hurry to return by lights-out."

Tom pulled his boots on and nodded. "Thanks for the concern, guys. I'll be back."

He rushed out the door, ducking items pelted at him by the guys as his boots clumped against the concrete floor. He pushed out the door and raced up the street. He paused at the rows of kennels.

The rows fanned in front of him. They had about thirteen hundred dogs right now, even though capacity was eighteen hundred. As many as four hundred fifty men could be on site, most of those being matched with dogs for training. So how could he be so concerned about one animal? Especially when it was a dog?

Those kinds of questions had no answers other than one girl. Only a girl like Lainie could make him do something that could jeopardize his career, if not his life.

He wasn't a doctor. He had no idea how to protect her until her body could heal. But as he'd prayed tonight, he knew with a certainty that he could do something by caring for Mason. If only he could do that away from a thousand dogs that were unknown risks.

"Thought I'd find you here." Sid sidled up next to Tom. "You are over the moon for her, aren't you?"

"What do you mean?"

"You never voluntarily come here. Only a woman could motivate you."

"You don't know what you're talking about." Tom blustered against the knowing in his heart that every word Sid spoke was true. He scanned the rows for Mason's kennel. He eased down the row until he saw her lying in front of it, ignoring the rest of the dogs. He pulled a treat from his pocket, and her ears perked. "Here you go, girl."

Mason leapt to her feet and accepted the rawhide. She took it to her kennel and sat down in the doorway, chewing on it.

Seeing Mason reminded Tom that he couldn't lose Lainie. Not when he'd just found her.

eighteen

June 28, 1943

The lecturer stepped away from the podium and took his seat. He'd droned on so long about military jargon that John Tyler, seated next to Tom, snored.

"All right, men. This is your last week of basic." Tired war whoops echoed Sergeant Maxwell's words. He glowered at them until quiet returned. Then he nodded. "Attention."

Chairs screeched against cement as soldiers bolted to their feet in the post theater. Tom tensed, staring straight ahead.

"Y'all think you're ready for war? We'll see what you think after today. Today's your introduction to the infiltration course. You must complete it in a satisfactory time before the end of the week." He stared down each man in the front row. Tom swallowed reflexively when Sarge locked eyes with him. "There are many ways to soldier. But I guarantee you will not survive the war without the skills you'll learn on the course. Move out."

Tom joined the others in a retreat to the loading area for the transport trucks that would carry them to the course. His stomach clenched as a rush of adrenaline spiked through him. He climbed into the back of a truck, stories he'd heard from the first round of trainees cycling through his mind. This course would be a rush unlike any he'd experienced. Designed to simulate combat, it would require him to apply everything he'd learned in the countless lectures and demonstrations.

Sam Donahue leaned across Tom and whistled at a pretty WAC walking toward the truck. He stood, arms crossed on the wood slats. "You our driver, beautiful?"

She rolled her eyes, tossed her hair, and smacked her gum.

"Honey, every guy here thinks I'm the girl for him. Get in line."

"Sit down, Romeo." Tom pulled on Sam's belt until he plopped down. The vehicle jerked into reverse, and she whipped the truck around before grinding into first gear and tearing down the road. The WAC acted as if they were already on the front lines of a war and she needed to avoid enemy bombers. Maybe that was part of the training, too.

Tom bounced against Sam on one side and John on the other as the truck hurtled up hills to the course. It lurched over another rock and slowed to a stop. Tom twisted to look over the cab. "So this is it."

"Looks that way." John pulled on his helmet and squared his jaw. "Let's finish this."

Sam rolled his eyes. "What's the rush? You know we'll do this again. Probably multiple times. Sarge Maxwell is having too much fun convincing us we ain't real soldiers. Can't wait for him to head back to his real base."

"Knowing our luck, he'll get reassigned. Here. Permanently." Sid's long face would have made actor Donald O'Connor proud.

"Let's tackle this before we worry about where he ends up." Tom jumped from the truck and walked over to where Sarge Maxwell waited, beefy arms crossed over his chest.

"All right, boys. Here we'll learn who's a real soldier. The rest of you can play army and hope you never leave Robinson. However, there's a war out there. One being fought across two oceans. This week you'll taste combat. Have fun." The glint in his eyes made Tom wonder how he defined fun.

Before he could spend too much time wondering, the men separated into platoons with sectors to cover. Tom approached the course in a crouch, head swiveling as he tried to find the front of the attack. Surely it couldn't be as simple as a direct frontal attack.

Whistling pierced the air to his right. Tom turned to follow the sound in time for the explosion. Its concussion knocked him off his feet. As more bombs whistled across the sky, Tom tried to sort out the range and types of weapons. It wasn't as easy as indicated in the lectures. He gave up and began digging a foxhole with his helmet.

"Get that helmet back on your head, Hamilton." Sarge barked the words in a tone that commanded Tom's obedience, even as he longed to burrow into the sandy earth.

❧

Lainie eyed the stack of books Tanya had brought from the library. Lainie couldn't focus on any of them long enough to read past the first chapter, not when images of the training Mason must be enduring filled her mind. Senseless romances weren't worth her time in the best of situations. Now she longed for anything to hold her attention. Distract her from the pain and Mason. Over the last week, the pain had eased, but it still lingered if she did more than walk across her room. Traveling to the first-floor parlor caused her joints to scream in protest.

Each spring in the couch seemed intent on gouging her skin. The blue-and-white floral-striped wallpaper had transformed the retreat into a prison cell. If she couldn't get out of the house soon, she'd go crazy.

The screen door slammed, and Lainie looked up to find Ginny Speares waltzing through the door. Her peaches-and-cream complexion was brighter than normal, and her auburn hair was damp around her face. "You've picked a good week to be confined indoors, Lainie." She clapped a hand over her mouth. "Oh, I'm sorry. That didn't come out the way I meant. It's an oven out there."

"It's not much cooler in here." Lainie forced a small smile. "Anything interesting at the post office?"

"Oh yes." Ginny reached into her pocket and pulled out an envelope.

Lainie grabbed the envelope and stared at the handwriting. It could only be a letter from Roxie Ottman, her roommate in Kentucky. She fumbled with the flap. The envelope trembled in her grasp, and she tried to swallow but couldn't.

Ginny reached for her. "You okay, Lainie? Is it bad news?"

"I think I'll read this in my room. Thanks, Ginny." Lainie stumbled out of the parlor.

When she reached her room, Lainie set the letter on the table and eased onto the bed. A tornado of emotions tore through her. She hadn't expected the anger that rushed through her. The passing months hadn't made her loss any less real. She tightened her jaw and squeezed her eyes shut. Even then, tears trickled down her cheeks. She rolled onto her pillow and buried her face in it as she sobbed.

Shadows danced across her bed. Lainie eyed them and wondered how long she'd slept. Her eyes felt crusted from her tears. And her soul felt emptied of hope. She turned toward the table and grimaced when she saw the envelope still sitting there. She'd wished it had been part of a dream. Why would Roxie write now?

She reached for the letter then pulled back. Was she ready to read about the adventures the girls had found in Italy?

Squaring her shoulders, she grabbed it and ripped the flap open. She unfolded the letter and brushed the folds smooth. Roxie's tiny script flowed across the page in even, narrow lines:

Dear Lainie,

We've arrived. You didn't miss much with the boat. Many of the gals spent days in their bunks as we bumped across every storm imaginable. I can't tell you how relieved I am to have solid land under my feet again.

We've only been in French Morocco a couple days, but I had to write. This is nothing like I imagined. I know you wanted to travel with us, but I think the doctors were right. This terrain is too harsh for someone recovering from an illness like yours.

Now, don't hate me for saying that. I know how angry you are. As I've prayed these weeks, I've prayed Isaiah 43 for you.

"Fear not, for I have redeemed you; I have summoned you by name; you are mine. When you pass through the waters, I will be with you; and when you pass through the rivers, they will not sweep over you. When you walk through the fire, you will not be burned; the flames will not set you ablaze. For I am the LORD, your God, the Holy One of Israel, your Savior. . . . Everyone who is called by my name, whom I created for my glory, whom I formed and made."

Lainie looked up from the letter and swiped at her cheeks. If only God felt that way about her. It was hard not to feel abandoned or overlooked. If God truly cared about her, why the pain of the last few months? Why the death of her dreams? Her heart ached at all she'd lost, and she rubbed over it, hoping to ease the pain.

Don't you see, Lainie? He created you and calls you His. He'll always be with you—no matter where you go or are sent. You are created for His glory. Don't you think you make Him smile just because? I love that thought. Especially on days it feels like there is so much more I should be doing.

Write soon, okay? Fill me in on all you're doing. I can't wait to hear. Knowing you, it will be something wonderful. You have a way of transforming what would paralyze others.

The girls say hi. Miss you, roomie.

Roxie

Lainie reread the letter, trying to soak in its spirit. She could picture Roxie penning it, tongue tucked between her lips as she concentrated on getting the words just right.

She reached for her Bible. There had to be more to Isaiah 43. Lainie felt a glimmer of hope. Maybe God did smile just because He'd made her and that was enough.

nineteen

July 5, 1943

Dr. Gibson pulled the stethoscope from around his neck and carefully placed it in his bag. Medical supplies bulged from the opening, and he brushed them aside to make room. When he finished, he tilted his head and stared at Lainie.

"Young lady, I'd say you're very fortunate. It appears your heart is unscathed, though we won't know for sure until you start your normal activities again."

Lainie slumped forward at the news. She'd braced herself for a far different prognosis. For the first time since the storm, she inhaled a breath and felt her lungs fill. His words echoed freedom to her.

"You can return to work on Monday, but I want you to stop the moment you feel a flicker of weakness."

"Yes, sir."

"Do I need to send Mrs. Babcock with you to ensure you obey my orders?"

"No. I promise I'll follow your instructions." Lainie clutched the neck of her nightgown, eager for him to leave.

"No more riding in rain storms. In fact, you should avoid anything strenuous for at least two weeks. We'll ease you back into the world with church and your job."

Her pulse raced at the thought of returning to church. With the last week in bed, she'd pondered Roxie's life-giving words. Lainie couldn't wait to join her voice with others as she thanked God for sparing her. She still didn't understand the whys, but she knew who. For now, she'd rest in His goodness. Even if He never showed her why she'd suffered, He deserved her love and worship.

Dr. Gibson grabbed his bag and stood. "Call me if you need anything else. Glad you're back on your feet."

"Thank you, Doctor." Lainie watched him go and wanted to twirl with her arms up in the air. Instead, she dressed and stumbled downstairs to the kitchen. Esther looked up from a pie she was crimping.

Lainie leaned against the counter. "Which kind are you making today?"

"Strawberry-rhubarb. I love the pucker of flavor the rhubarb adds."

Lainie grimaced at the memory of the last strawberry-rhubarb pie she'd carried. Mason's image flashed in her mind. "Doc Gibson says I've recovered. Maybe I can find out what's happened to Mason. See if anything's changed."

Esther eyed her. "That's not exactly what he said."

"Maybe, but if I can leave, why not go there? Much as I like my room and appreciate your patience with me, I'm ready to see something else." Anything else, really.

"Then you can eat down here tonight." Esther's jaw set in a determined line, and Lainie sighed. This Esther she couldn't cross or persuade. She might as well accept that she was stuck here until Monday.

Lainie shrugged. Maybe a special soldier would stop by. Tom Hamilton had come to check on her periodically. He'd been the only soldier to do so, and the action made her appreciate him even more. He was unlike the other men she'd grown up with or met here. He cared and wasn't afraid to show it, yet somehow it didn't diminish him at all. Indeed, he seemed stronger because of it.

She wondered at her reaction. How could she care so much about a man she'd known less than two months? No man had ever caught her attention like Tom, yet many had tried. Somehow none had interested her enough to get a second or third look. No, she enjoyed dancing with and entertaining soldiers the best. Until she'd arrived at Fort Robinson, she'd never had to consider more than a fleeting moment with a man. Even back home Roger had always been a friend. Here, most stayed the eight to twelve weeks that training with the dogs required. Then there was Tom and the rest of the cadre that stayed.

"You need something else, Lainie?"

Lainie jerked, startled from her thoughts, and looked at Esther. The twinkle in Esther's eyes could power the lights in town. Heat climbed Lainie's cheeks, and she shook her head. "No, I think I'll sit on the porch for a while. See you at supper."

"See you then." Esther's chuckle followed Lainie as she left the room.

❧

This was it. Tom wiped a stream of sweat from under his helmet and adjusted his pack. Even after six weeks, it rested heavily against his back and pulled his shoulders, which were knotted tight as cords of wood.

Boots smacked along the hardened trail. Scorching heat from the sun pounded against his helmet, and a trickle of sweat slipped down his face. He squinted up the trail to gauge the remaining distance to the Wood Reserve. Tom tried to focus on the trail and God's creation that dotted the path. Pockets of sandwort stacked claims among the rocks. He stepped around a stand of plains prickly pear that had edged onto the trail. The bright yellow flowers couldn't hide the long barbs of that cactus, one he'd learned the hard way to avoid.

The men entered a clearing and pulled to a halt.

"Ten-hut." Sarge Maxwell strutted to the front of the group. "You're some of the sorriest excuses for soldiers I've seen, but I guess you'll do. You've completed basic training and are now free from the hikes and packs until sent elsewhere."

A murmur moved through the ranks, an echo of the relief Tom felt. He'd earned his marksmanship badge and actually looked forward to spending time with the dogs and avoiding senseless drills. Tomorrow he'd wear his cowboy boots rather than the standard-issue boots he had the blisters to prove he'd worn the last six weeks.

"First, form up. Time to show us some drills."

The men marched in tight formation around the field until Maxwell grunted his approval. He stuck an unlit cigar between his teeth and grimaced. "Form up for inspection."

Tom swiped a drink from his canteen and fell in between Sid and John. Maxwell dragged out the inspection until Tom's muscles tensed with fatigue. The man seemed to delight in finding something, anything, to nag each soldier about. Tom wouldn't miss Maxwell, and his anger, one bit.

Eventually Maxwell released them, and Sergeant Lewis replaced him at the front. Sarge considered the ranks in front of him carefully.

"At ease." He took off pacing in front of them. "I have to say I'm pleased with the way you have performed during basic. Despite Sergeant Maxwell's bluster, he's given me favorable reports of many of your efforts and improvements. Congratulations. Tomorrow we'll return to our routine. Today, however, break into your platoons for field events." He grinned at them. "Don't forget, the winning platoon will be wined and dined by the rest tonight."

Tom groaned; he'd hoped to slip by Mrs. Babcock's and check on Lainie. He thrust his pack into the growing pile by a truck and entered the events. The balance of the day flew past in a rush of races and contests. At the end of the competition, his platoon fell a bit short.

"The officers judging the long jump really need new glasses," Sid grumbled as he marched toward the roaring bonfire.

"And what about the dash? Come on—all you have to do is operate a stopwatch." John rolled his eyes. "Guess we'll have to remember I was the fastest man on the field today."

Tom walloped both men on the shoulder. "It's over now. Let's enjoy the end of basic."

In no time, they joined the men gathered around the fire. Soon a soldier launched into a song, and others joined. Tom's tension eased as he watched the hundred or so men around him kick back and celebrate the successful completion of basic. Now all were ready to serve wherever the army determined they'd make the most difference in this war. As he considered the men gathered around the fire, he knew he would trust his life to any of them. They were trained and primed, even though many would serve out the war at Robinson.

Wood smoke filled his nose, and Tom's thoughts wandered to the many nights he and his father had sat around a fire, staring at stars too numerous to count. Dad had often been busy with his practice, but at least twice a year, they'd retreat to the mountains. Each day had ended like this one.

"Hey." A voice cut across the singing. "We're under attack. Grab your weapons!"

Tom rolled out of the way as the men around him erupted to their feet. He looked through the lowering light. Where was the truck with his pack? He sprang to his feet and dashed across the space.

He unfastened his rifle and tried to remember if it was loaded. There hadn't been any shooting drills today, so no need to load. He grabbed a box of shells from the pack and cast the pack aside. He loaded the gun as he ran to find the rest of his platoon. They formed a perimeter around one flank of the fire.

Tom searched the darkness for any sign of whoever had assaulted their position. The sound of scuffling filled the air from pockets outside the light of the fire. Gunfire erupted, and Tom dove for the dirt, landing next to Sid.

"What?"

"I don't know." Sid's face held a crazed look. "Keep looking. We can't be the weak point."

Tom turned back to the perimeter. The explosion of an artillery shell shook the ground, and he started digging a foxhole with his bare hands. He scanned the horizon as he dug, throwing the dirt in front of him.

Shadows rushed across the edge of the trees, but he couldn't find a clear line of sight. The sun sank behind the buttes, and the actions of the platoons became more organized as a messenger ran between them with instructions. Tom's blood pounded an intense beat in his ears, and his finger trembled on the trigger.

"I see them," John Tyler bellowed in Tom's ear.

"I've got them." Tom followed their progress down the barrel of his rifle. It was loaded with live ammunition, and he didn't want to injure a friend. This had to be part of a drill. Taking a deep breath, Tom considered his options then aimed over the encroachers' heads. He eased back on the trigger and grinned when they dove for the ground.

A shrill whistle pierced the air, loud enough to drown out intermittent blasts.

"All right, men." Corporal Hill's voice blasted through a megaphone. Tom's shoulders relaxed. The drill was over. "Congratulations on defending your posts and completing basic training. Enjoy the balance of your evening, but don't forget reveille sounds at 0530."

Groans mixed with whoops as the men gathered around the fire.

Tom stowed his rifle back with his pack and then leaned against it as he watched the fun. Now maybe life could return to normal. And maybe he could show Lainie how much she meant to him. A smile grew on his face. He knew just how to do it.

twenty

It looked as though he had everything. Now Tom needed the day to end so he could launch his plan. He settled the picnic basket under the instructor's desk in the lecture hall. The hall was empty, as most men were in the middle of field drills with their dogs. Tom would rather be with them enjoying the fresh air. Instead, he was shackled to the desk until he caught up on paperwork he'd ignored during basic.

Mary in the war dog office had confirmed that Lainie would return to work today. He couldn't wait to see her. The last weeks had been too long between the demands of basic and Mrs. Babcock's overprotectiveness. Maybe Lainie needed rest, but isolation?

Tom focused on the paperwork in front of him. He had dozens of evaluation forms to complete before he could leave. Then he faced stacks of examinations to grade. Those would be his excuse to drop by and see Lainie. Not that he needed an excuse if she felt the same about him. If absence really made the heart grow fonder and all that.

He pulled his attention back to the record in front of him. Pepper and his trainer, Will Green, had turned into a good team. Over the last two weeks of war dog basic training, they had bonded into a unit. Pepper looked to Green for approval and obeyed without question. Green had picked up the key skills in caring for and training his dogs to obey and respect him. Tom filled in the dog training record with *h*'s to reflect Pepper's high degree of intelligence, willingness, energy, aggressiveness, and sensitivity. Flipping to Green's personnel record, he pulled out the practical tests, made sure all were completed, and added a couple of remarks. Green, with his patience and quickness, would make a good instructor if needed.

Tom worked through several forms before looking up and stretching his arms over his head. Paperwork had to be the worst thing about the army. He rolled his neck and turned back to the slowly shrinking stack.

John burst into the room. "Why are you sitting there? Come on. You have to see this."

"See what?" Tom continued to fill in a form, this one on Rocky. Where did people get the names for their dogs? What did a dog have in common with a rock?

"The airfield. It's amazing to watch the engineers build it."

"Can't or Sergeant Lewis will have my hide. See this stack? I've hardly dented it."

"It'll be there tomorrow. At the rate the strip is going in, it might be done by then." John's arms waved as he described the huge machines leveling the land and rolling out the concrete. "You have to come."

Tom evaluated the stack. It had shrunk. And a few minutes wouldn't matter overall. Then he thought of Lainie and the picnic basket tucked under the desk. No, he had to finish. "You'll have to fill me in. Though how are you finding the time to watch? You must be buried, too."

"Nope. That's the beauty of working in processing. The vets have to handle the paperwork. All I have to do is help with each animal."

"Get out of here." Tom shooed him away and shook his head. Some guys had all the luck. A job without paperwork. A beautiful bride. Maybe someday. . .but not if he didn't get this done.

♣

Lainie watched the clock on the far wall of the office all afternoon, praying the hands would spin faster. Each minute seemed bogged down in the throbbing ache that had settled over her. This morning she'd been eager to escape the prison bars Mrs. Babcock had developed. Now all she could think about was slipping between the sheets of her bed.

"Here, Lainie." Mary placed a steaming mug of coffee on her desk. "It's got sugar and milk the way you like."

"Thanks."

"Maybe it will help."

Lainie could only nod as tears clouded her sight.

"Hey, it's okay. You're here, and I, for one, missed you." Mary squeezed her shoulders and moved back to her desk.

Lainie scanned the room. Not all the girls felt the same as Mary. Kate had ignored her completely, while Rae Beth and Kitty seemed indifferent to see her back. Almost as if they thought the fever would spread to them. They should know the army wouldn't let her back until both her doctor and the base hospital had cleared her.

Why waste her breath explaining? Either they understood or they didn't. Little she could say would change their minds. Though part of her wished she could.

She flexed her fingers and wrists, trying to ease the stiffness and soreness. During the morning, she'd filed papers and had the cuts to prove it. After lunch, the typewriter had demanded her attention. She picked up the warm mug of coffee and curled her fingers around it. Maybe the warmth would ease the stiffness. She sipped the brew. Mary had added enough sugar and milk to make it drinkable.

The steady beat of the clock ticking reminded her that the stack of correspondence wouldn't shrink on its own. Reluctantly she returned the mug to the desk and moved the first letter closer to the typewriter. She groaned as she read that another dog had died from distemper. She had to get Mason away.

Swiveling in the chair, Lainie began to type the standard letter:

It is with much regret that we inform you of the death of your dog, Bully, whom you so generously donated through

Dogs for Defense for use by the armed forces. A war dog certificate is forwarded herewith. A mere certificate of death is, indeed, poor compensation for your patriotic sacrifice, and the Army is not unaware of it. We, too, are sorry to lose so prominent an animal and assure you that your generosity is sincerely appreciated.

Tears trailed down her cheeks, but she typed anyway, determined to finish this letter and the next. She must prove she could handle the work.

Finally, the day ended. Lainie didn't think she could handle many more letters to owners about the demise of their dogs. Next time she'd have to ask Mary to help her. With each letter, she pictured Mason's name. Maybe tomorrow she'd try to check on her, confirm she was okay. By now, Mason must be past basic training and probably intermediate, too. What specialized training had the army assigned her to? None of the options seemed good.

Lainie could imagine Mason's terror as she heard guns and artillery. Each day, the instructors brought the sound nearer, making the caliber of the gun larger, until all dogs were inured to the sound.

The girls collected their hats and bags. Lainie stood to join them in the walk to the shuttle. She squared her shoulders and raised her chin. No need to carry her fears with her. She walked out the door and stopped. The most beautiful sight leaned against the side of his car. The smile started deep inside her until it spread to her lips. "Hey."

"Hi, beautiful. Your chariot awaits." Tom gestured toward his car and then stepped toward her and offered a hand.

Rae Beth and Kate tittered as they looked over their shoulders at Tom. For once, Lainie didn't care what they thought.

"I've missed you, Tom."

"Me, too. Come with me?" The question in his eyes compelled her even as she nodded, her words swept away by his nearness. He opened the passenger door then settled her in the car as if she were priceless china.

The aroma of ham and spicy mustard mixed in the air. Tom slid behind the wheel.

"It smells good."

"I thought we'd enjoy a picnic if you're up to it. Maybe find a spot to watch the sunset and count the stars." He stared at her with such intensity that Lainie had to look away. "Lainie, I was so worried, and Mrs. Babcock wouldn't let me see you. Should you be back? Are you recovered?"

She touched her fingers to his lips and stilled his words. He held his breath. "Dr. Gibson and the base physician both say I'm fine. I'll need to be careful and have been warned to expect dire consequences if I let this happen again. God sheltered me, though I don't know why."

Tom pressed her fingers against his lips and kissed them. "I'm so relieved. The little that Mrs. Babcock told me painted horrible pictures in my mind." He turned away, breaking the intensity, and exhaled. "Let's find a place to catch up and eat."

Easy conversation filled the car as Tom took them down dirt road after dirt road. Lainie didn't even try to figure out where they were headed. Instead, she enjoyed the mystery and the company.

As she watched Tom, she doubted anyone else could compel her attention. He was more than she deserved. Steady, unflappable, committed, with a heart that chased God's. She whispered a prayer of thanks. Only God could orchestrate a friendship like theirs. And maybe, just maybe, there was more. She'd known him only two months, but it was enough time to learn his character.

Tom pulled the car to the side of the road. "Here we are."

"I won't even ask where that is."

A wry grin creased his face. "If you're lucky, I'll find our way home."

"Hmm. I see your plan. Take the sick woman to the middle of nowhere. Feed her and then lose her. Sounds like a delightful evening." Lainie stuck out her tongue at him.

Later Lainie lay on a blanket, watching vibrant colors paint the sky as the sun slipped below the horizon. The picnic had been perfect when she ignored the ache in her muscles. The evening was worth it. She shivered as a night breeze blew, and Tom tucked a blanket around her.

"We should get you home."

She sat up and nodded. Much as she'd like to stay, he was right. He tipped her chin up. Heat slipped up her cheeks, and she held her breath. He leaned toward her and then waited, as if asking permission. She slipped her arms around his neck, and his lips found hers.

In that moment, all she could imagine was a future with Tom, filled with nights like this.

He pulled away and searched her face. "I think I love you, Lainie Gardner."

twenty-one

July 8, 1943

Lainie floated into the war dog office, a basket of Esther's muffins tucked under her arm. "Get them while they're hot, girls."

She watched the girls enjoy the muffins and knew the day would be wonderful. Her lips still tingled from Tom's kiss, and she didn't think she'd ever forget the feeling of being tucked so safely under his arm or hearing his words. While not a firm confession of love, they matched her feelings. This might be love. But they needed time to explore it.

The morning flew by as she prepared honorable discharge papers for dogs that had failed some aspect of basic training. Not every dog sent to the fort met the army's requirements. Some were too short, others too aggressive, and still others too distracted by anything that moved. Why couldn't wonderful Mason be any of those things? Of course, she would take to the instruction like a prairie dog to the hills. It was decidedly unfair.

Lainie shook her head and forced her thoughts back to Tom. Time to think about better things. Something she could control.

"You look far away." Mary leaned over the typewriter to see the stack of papers. "I know it's not the paperwork. Not with that smile."

A grin softened Lainie's face. "You're right. It's good to be back."

Mary chuckled. "Sure it is, honey. Don't worry. I have a feeling your soldier will be by soon. That man lights up around you."

"Let's just say last night was wonderful, and I hope he does come by soon. I already miss him."

"I think that qualifies for over the moon."

Kitty snorted. "Sappy's what I'd call it."

Lainie made a face and stuck out her tongue at the girl. Then she turned back to her typing and tuned out the girls' conversations. Not hard to do when her thoughts kept returning to a rock under the clear night sky.

≈

Tom watched another group of men parade their dogs through close-order drills. The dogs heeled like well-oiled machines. They kept an eye cocked on their masters and followed the silent hand signals without a hitch. Time for the next challenge.

"All right, men. Close ranks."

The groups shuffled into position, forming straight rows. One dog growled in the back of its throat, and Tom searched the lines until he saw the animal. Brutus had an attitude problem that kept him in the program—barely. And only because Sergeant Prescott had firm control of the animal. Prescott looked at him and nodded.

"I've got him under control, sir."

Tom watched the dog. Brutus's ears remained swiveled to the side, but his hackles had begun to settle. Satisfied, Tom did a quick inspection of the teams. Mason sat two dogs down from Brutus. Despite Lainie's concerns, Mason thrived in the army. She'd picked up each new command quickly and showed an intelligence that would make her an asset wherever she served. She'd been paired with an army air soldier, so her destination was unsure.

"Since you've mastered the on-leash drills, we'll move to off-leash exercises. When I command, spread out then release your dogs. Make them remain at your side. We'll run through some familiar commands to see how they do without the leash encouraging obedience. If all goes well, we'll reward them with a round of the obstacle course."

A cheer rose from the marines. Leave it to marines to love the idea of crawling through mud, leaping over obstacles, and running until you couldn't see through the sweat. From the odor blowing his way, it smelled as though many of them had already run several miles.

"Separate." Tom waited until the men had spread out with enough space between them to keep each dog focused on its master. "Unleash your dogs and review *sit*, *stay*, and *down* with them."

He walked among the rows, checking for any signs that a dog had readied to bolt. The last thing they needed this week was another dog or two going AWOL. The last one had finally been roped down by a former rodeo star who now served with the veterinary corp. And that was only after several men on horseback had chased the dog all over the parade grounds and the other side of the highway.

A deep growl pulled Tom's attention back to Brutus. The dog looked ready to spring. "Prescott, grab him." Tom barked the order and prayed.

Brutus's ears were pinned against his head, his teeth bared, and he'd crouched. Another growl rumbled, this one louder.

"Prescott!" Tom rubbed his scar. Nothing would happen to Prescott on his watch.

The man stood as if paralyzed, staring at his dog. Tom caught movement to Prescott's right and watched it out of the corner of his eye as he marched toward Prescott. Teams around the two put distance between them, all except for Mason and her owner. Tom grimaced. Private Rush and Prescott had developed a friendship, and it looked as though Rush wanted to intervene.

"Back away, Rush."

The man ignored him, easing toward Prescott. "Come on, buddy. Snap out of it. You've got to move. Now."

Prescott shook his head. Brutus followed his movements then looked at Rush and Mason. Mason followed Rush, still off-leash. The dog was too well trained and obedient for her own safety. Brutus launched at Mason and wrestled her to the ground, teeth sinking into her neck.

"No!" Tom screamed the word and raced toward the two. How could he disable Brutus long enough to pull him away without shooting? Mason fought back, but her size was no match for Brutus's. Tom froze, watching them war, flashes of a former dog fight blazing across his mind. He rubbed his scar again then shook his head. Mason didn't deserve this mauling. He pulled his sidearm out of its holster and aimed.

A soft whistle whizzed past his ear, and a tranquilizer dart sank into Brutus's flank. The dog's actions slowed; then he collapsed on top of Mason. Tom tore his eyes from the mess of dogs to the vet tech who raced up.

"Took you long enough to get here."

"I'm here now. Let's get these two separated and to the hospital stat. We may be able to save the black one."

Two more vet techs raced up in a Jeep. It took them several minutes to pry Brutus off of Mason and get her loaded. Rush and Prescott boarded the Jeep with their dogs and disappeared down the hill toward the vet hospital. Tom rubbed his hand over his face. What was he going to tell Lainie? This was exactly what she'd feared from the moment Mason arrived. He didn't think he could tell her, but he knew he couldn't let her find out from someone else.

He turned back to the remaining teams. The men waited, their dogs lounging at their sides. "Run through the obstacle course a couple times. Nobody's hiding along the course, so focus on clearing the barriers." He turned and followed the Jeep. The men would have to follow instructions without a babysitter.

When he reached the hospital a few minutes later, the techs had already whisked Mason away. All he could learn was she still lived. For now, that would have to be enough.

He stepped outside and took several deep breaths, trying to clear the heavy antiseptic smell from his lungs. He looked across the road. Less than one hundred feet separated him from Lainie. He had to tell her. Now. Even though he wanted to deliver any message but this one.

❧

"Hey, Lainie. Look who's here." Kitty's voice pulled Lainie's attention from a file.

Lainie's heart skipped to a faster tempo. She curved her lips in a smile. "Hi, Tom."

He pulled his hat off and twisted it in his hands. He shuffled from side to side, and a bad feeling spread through Lainie.

"What is it?"

Emotions warred across his face. First a flash of concern. Then a tightening around his eyes and jaw. Followed by a visible effort to relax.

"Spit it out." She looked at her hands, surprised to see them trembling.

"Could you come outside for a moment?" He swallowed then looked into her, through her. "Please, Lainie."

She glanced around the room, and Mary nodded, so she slipped from behind the desk and walked out as Tom held the door for her. She wrapped her arms around herself and turned on him.

"What happened? You're scaring me to death. Did you change your mind about last night?"

A flash of relief lit up his face. "No, nothing like that. Last night was wonderful. It's about Mason." He spoke the last sentence so softly Lainie leaned forward to catch the words.

"Did you say Mason?"

Tom nodded.

Lainie dashed in front of a truck and across the street. The driver honked his horn, but she kept running. She stumbled up the few steps to the door and pulled it open. "Please, God."

Tears tumbled down her cheeks as she whispered the words. Nothing could have happened to Mason. Not the sweet, obedient dog. She'd never done anything wrong in her life other than chewing one of Mama's tables in a fit of boredom. But that was years ago.

"I knew this would happen."

A man sat behind a desk in front of her. She skirted around it, but he stood to block her way. "Miss, you can't go back there."

Lainie pounded against his chest. "My dog is in there. I have to see her."

"You can't go back there." His gaze softened. "Take the chair over there, and I'll let you know when we know something. Which dog is yours?"

Which? More than one was hurt? She had to get Mason out of here.

twenty-two

Lainie sat on her bed, staring at her reflection in the mirror on her wardrobe. Her face had a new brittle quality to it. It seemed to have settled there when she learned about Mason. She'd waited what seemed like hours for any word. At some point Tom had joined her, but she couldn't bring herself to acknowledge him. If he'd helped like she'd asked, Mason would be back in North Platte where she belonged rather than in some strange hospital.

Her mind replayed image after image of times spent with Mason. Each made her think of home and safety. Then the scent of bleach and cleaners that had assaulted her when she entered the hospital overwhelmed her. She didn't know if she'd ever get rid of that awful smell.

This morning Tom had come by again to tell her the vets thought Mason would recover.

"Let me take you over there to see her," he had cajoled her, but she couldn't.

Her stomach turned at the thought that Mason would recover, and she'd almost lost her breakfast. How could she explain to Tom that the last thing she wanted was Mason permanently injured? But if she was, then at least she'd be discharged. Instead, she'd recover and remain in the army.

"I can't go over there now. Maybe over lunch." Fresh tears had washed her cheeks, and Lainie had done nothing to wipe them away.

Tom had tried to pull her into his embrace, but Lainie had pushed him away. Her emotions rocked all over. With one breath, she had loved his sweetness. With the next, she wanted to hold him accountable for what had happened. Even though someone had told her he'd been ready to jump into the fray.

"Please leave me alone. I. . .I need some time to think." Time to prepare another plan to free Mason. There had to be a way before she was killed.

Confusion had clouded Tom's expression, but he'd backed toward the door. Then he was gone. Lainie had sunk to her chair and ignored the other girls' stares. Mary had knelt in front of her.

"Are you okay, Lainie?"

"No." Fresh tears erupted into sobs. Mary hugged her as Lainie cried. What had she done? Would Tom abandon her now? She wouldn't blame him. Slowly she collected her thoughts. She straightened and sniffed while she dabbed her eyes with a handkerchief. "Thanks, but we both have work to do."

"Take a few minutes to see Mason. It'll do you good."

Lainie had, and now as she looked in the mirror, she wished she hadn't. Mason had been sedated, the hair shaved from around her neck and a large bandage swathed around one part of it. She'd whimpered in her sleep, her front legs jerking as if chasing a bunny.

"Oh, Mason."

Lainie squared her shoulders and reached for the red dress that Audrey loved so much. A slight smile flitted across her face at the memory of Audrey trying it on and deciding it was too much for her red hair. Lainie had no such problems. A yoked waist and pleated skirt set off the cap sleeves and gathered bodice. It would be perfect when paired with her black pumps for the K-9 dance.

She didn't feel like a night out but knew she couldn't stay home and mope. She reached for her new bottle of stocking lotion and brushed it along her legs. She eyed the color, pleased it looked so much like hose. When it dried, she slipped on her dress. She patted some powder on her face and reached for her lipstick.

Dorothy stuck her head around the door. "Ready, Lainie? The guys are here."

For a moment, Lainie wished Tom was the one taking her, but she'd turned him away. How much fun would she be tonight anyway between an aching heart and body? She had to get her emotions under control before she could spend more time with Tom. She couldn't see him without seeing Mason, and that wasn't fair to him.

She swiped the lipstick on and hurried after Dorothy.

The tennis courts had been transformed. Someone had strung soft Christmas lights along the fence. Chinese lanterns, streamers, and balloons festooned every surface. Tables were set up immediately outside the courts and loaded with finger sandwiches and desserts. The sun hung in the sky as if kissing the event with its warmth and light.

Dorothy and Tanya disappeared into the mass with their dates. Lainie smiled at the transformation in Tanya. She'd cut her hair and bought new clothes. Even though they were from Sears, they'd wrought a change in her outlook, and that had changed her social schedule.

Lainie walked toward the food but was stopped by a soldier.

"Dance with me, miss?" The clean-cut young man had a youthful energy.

"I'd be delighted."

Song after song, soldiers stepped up to twirl her around the floor. Occasionally she accepted their offers. More often she invited them to sit with her. From each, she coaxed stories and loved to watch smiles light up their faces as they talked about home and sometimes the girl waiting for them. The music finally ended when the band took a break.

"Ladies and gentleman, if you'll clear the center of the floor, we will have a demonstration by Private Newman and his dog, Lucky."

Lainie watched with wonder as the dog ran through his tricks. The dog seemed to count as he tapped his foot on the court to answer questions from his master. Then they ran through a series of commands. It was amazing.

All too soon, the show ended. The sun had left a veil of darkness in its place. The sound of crickets filled the air now that the musicians and partygoers were silent. She searched the dwindling crowd for Dorothy and Tanya but couldn't find them. Lainie started walking the perimeter of the courts, looking for her ride. Tom leaned against his car as if waiting for her. She froze then took a step toward him.

He looked good in his dress uniform with sharp pleats and buffed shoes, as though he'd dressed up for the dance, yet she hadn't seen him there. He pushed off the car and strolled toward her.

"Can I give you a lift?"

Lainie swallowed against the fist of anger that had lodged in her throat. Was it only two nights earlier that she'd listened to him murmur that he loved her and prayed that it was true? That her heart had begun to race at such a pace that she'd wondered if it would ever calm? His blue eyes had deepened to almost black, intensity pulsing from him.

A glance revealed her ride still hadn't appeared. With that, she had no option but to accept. "All right, Tom. Thank you."

He took her hand and settled her in the car. Awkward silence filled the air as Tom drove. He cleared his throat and glanced at her. "I've talked to Sarge about Mason. He says if she's going to recover, she has to stay in the army."

"I know."

"I'm working on it, Lainie. Don't give up."

"I wish somebody had acted before she was almost mauled to death."

The car slowed as Tom drove off the highway and into town. "I'm sorry, but I tried everything I could to stop the attack. Why aren't you mad at the folks who sent her here?"

She fought that question. How could her dad be so callous? She longed to throw herself in Tom's arms and listen to him tell her everything would be okay. Another part longed to lash out at him even though he didn't deserve it. Instead, she counted houses until they reached Mrs. Babcock's. She opened the door before he could turn off the engine. "Thanks for the ride."

All night, the picture of Tom's openmouthed surprise at her behavior plagued her. Why lash out at him? If adversity shows what one is made of, she didn't like what her sickness and the scare with Mason revealed about her. She swiped away another tear as she sat on the edge of her bed and stared out the window. She tried to count stars, but tears blurred her vision.

God, I need help. Please show me that You care about me, because right now I feel pretty overlooked.

ॐ

Sunday morning, Lainie strolled with Esther and the other girls through Crawford's streets until they reached First Christian Church. She waited for the others to slide into a pew two-thirds of the way back in the sanctuary before slipping in. She smoothed her skirt and adjusted her beret. Hollowness seemed to choke her as she looked around the small room. She felt like a child who'd lost her daddy at a large fair. She could spin in a circle looking for him but not see him in the crush of people.

Where had God gone? Since her illness in Kentucky, she'd felt as though she searched for Him in a heavy fog, and He chose not to be found. She'd thought He cared about her. Now she wondered. She mouthed the words to the hymns and went through the motions of the service, her heart searching for an answer.

Pastor Stevenson stepped to the podium and gazed across the group. "A couple weeks ago, I talked about the passage in Isaiah 43 where God promises He has redeemed us and will walk with us through trials of all sorts.

"This is a hard concept to grasp, yet foundational to faith. Does God mean what He says? Is His word the same in Isaiah's day and today? And why would God care enough to reassure us of His presence and redemption? Because without Him we are nothing. We are desperate creatures in need of God to save us.

"If you feel abandoned by God, I assure you He is there. You may not see Him or sense Him, but it doesn't change the fact that He is still there."

Lainie felt a flicker of hope at the pastor's words.

"Look for Him. Ask Him to open your eyes to His movement on your behalf. I am convinced that if you do, your perspective will be transformed."

Peace teased Lainie as she listened, seeming beyond her grasp. God was with her. She knew that in her head. He had to be, since He promised. But her heart wondered. So much had happened this year, good and bad. Would He reveal Himself? She'd been so sure after getting Roxie's letter. How could she reclaim that peace and certainty?

twenty-three

July 13, 1943

Tom rushed out the door of the training center and raced toward the K-9 office. He banged through the door without stopping to knock.

"Lainie, grab your purse and meet me at the vet hospital in ten minutes."

She stared at him with a slack jaw, as did the other girls in the office. He couldn't wait to see if she'd take him seriously. There was too much to do if this was going to work.

Sarge had had a change of heart over the weekend, and Tom wasn't going to give him time to reconsider. He raced to his car and checked the gas gauge. Full. Good, they wouldn't have to stop for gas. Next, he ran to the barracks and grabbed his duffle. He tossed in a couple of extra uniforms and other essentials before zipping it shut. He threw the bag over his shoulder and ran to the office to collect his pass. He had three days on a Class A pass. It would be rushed but should be enough time. Now if Lainie would cooperate.

When he reached the kennel and hospital, Lainie waited at the door. He paused to stare at her after shutting off his car. Her hair was pulled back at the nape of her neck with a simple ribbon. She wore a blouse, sweater, skirt, and saddle shoes. A simple outfit that somehow managed to highlight her beauty.

He climbed out of the car, reached into his back pocket, and pulled out a sheet of paper. This was it. "Follow me, mademoiselle."

She looked at him quizzically but twined her arm through his. "All right."

"I hold in my hot little hand Mason's get-out-of-jail-free card.

We're taking her home."

Lainie squealed and threw her arms around his neck. She laughed and cried at the same time. After a minute, she pulled back from him. "Are you sure, Tom?"

"Absolutely, but I only have three days to help you get her home. So let's hurry. Time's wasting."

The next hour passed in a blur of completing Mason's paperwork, taking Lainie to Mrs. Babcock's, and waiting for her to pack. Finally, they were all settled in his Chevy, Mason stretched out in back and Lainie sitting next to Tom.

"Yesterday I asked God to show me that He saw me. And now this. After everything I tried to do, all the people I talked to. Just like that, Mason is coming home." She tucked her head against his shoulder. "Thank you, Tom."

Warmth filled him. It wasn't often God used Tom and a dog to show His love. But God had changed him, too, in so many good ways. "My fear's gone, Lainie. I'm not necessarily ready to befriend any dog I meet, but I don't feel the need to keep an eye on Mason or defend myself from her."

"That's wonderful." Lainie bit her lip but kept her eyes on the road. "I wish I could keep Mason here."

"Mrs. Babcock won't let you?"

"No. She's got a strict no-animal policy. Says she can't have them with the restaurant." Lainie seemed to collapse inside herself, the excitement of getting Mason muted by something.

"What is it?"

"I wish I knew how my family will react. I couldn't reach them on the phone, so our arrival will be a surprise. Dad doesn't do well with surprises, especially when he thinks things are already set." A smile touched her lips. "I guess I'll have to believe that this will work out somehow."

The miles passed as he got her talking about her family and friends. The afternoon melted away with a quick stop in Alliance followed by another one for fuel in Ogallala. Just when he thought they would never arrive, they reached North Platte.

"Mama should be home, but Daddy's probably at the bank."

"Don't bankers keep regular hours? It's after five."

"Not Daddy. He has a hard time allowing someone else to take care of things. It's probably why the bank stayed solvent during the Depression, but it made for a lonely house."

Tom followed Lainie's directions to her home. He pulled the car into the circular driveway. The brick home had classic lines with a wide porch. The landscaping was lush even in the July heat. He'd known she came from a well-off family, but this was more.

"Let's get inside. I'm eager to introduce you to Mama. Then we can go down to Wahl's for a Coke, maybe see a movie." Lainie reached for Mason's harness and leash and helped her out of the car. Her steps slowed as she approached the front door. She looked back at Tom. "Here we go."

Tom grabbed their bags and followed her. Ready or not, it was time to meet her parents.

Mrs. Gardner welcomed him warmly through her surprise. Tom liked the vision of what Lainie would look like in twenty-five years. Little would change other than a light touch of gray in her hair.

"Lainie, why don't you get Mason reintroduced to the backyard before your father gets home? I'll show Tom here to your rooms."

Lainie quirked an eyebrow at him as if asking if he'd be okay. He tried to shoo her on, but the bags hampered him.

"I hope you don't mind the visit, Mrs. Gardner. We had to jump when the army agreed to release Mason."

"Not at all. You must be tired after that drive. I'm surprised you didn't take the train." She gestured into the room at the top of the stairs. "This will be your room while you're with us."

Tom tossed his bag next to the bed in the darkening room. "Thank you."

She appraised him then nodded. "Yes. I think we'll enjoy your visit. This way."

Lainie's bedroom was past her parents', and then they took a back stairway down to the kitchen. Lainie returned with an unharnessed Mason, peace softening her features even as something kept her eyes tight. Tom caught his breath at the sight. There was a hint of promise about her, too. Before he could ask her about it, the front door flew open.

"Where's my little lady?"

Mrs. Gardner blushed as she rushed down the hall. A big bear of a man waited for her. Tom found it hard to believe he was dainty Lainie's father. Lainie caught his gaze and rolled her eyes.

"Someday they'll grow out of it, but they refuse."

"I hope my wife is that excited to see me twenty years after we're married."

"Try twenty-eight. It's almost scandalous." Her face formed into a mask of mock horror. "Let's slip out the back."

"Oh no, you don't. I've waited to meet your father."

Loud steps echoed down the wooden hallway. "I see you've brought home a soldier and Mason. I must say, I expected more of you, baby doll."

"What did you expect me to do? Leave her with the army after she was injured? I tried to tell you this would happen."

"Still full of passion, aren't we? She's a dog. Sometimes you forget that. Come here." The man hugged a stiff Lainie then shook hands with Tom and examined him. "Mr. Gardner, son. Mama, what's for dinner?"

With that, Tom had a perfect understanding that he was not the man Lainie's father wanted for his daughter. He glanced at Lainie and knew she'd seen it, too. She shrugged and hooked her arm through Tom's.

"I'm taking Tom downtown tonight. We can only stay tomorrow and then have to return to Crawford. Mom, we didn't get a chance to warn you we were coming, so we'll slip out. You and Dad have a great dinner, and we'll catch up with you later." She pulled Tom down the hallway. "Don't wait up."

Tom looked back and caught Mr. Gardner's face contorted

in a grimace, and Mrs. Gardner holding him back. "They'll be fine, Bob."

"Quit looking at them, and let's get out of here." Lainie's voice was pitched higher than usual. "Come on."

"We should spend time with them."

"We will. Later. We'll wait until my sister, Betty, is a buffer. I'll show you bustling North Platte tonight."

Tom let her direct him the few blocks to downtown. They parked in front of a small diner and went inside. Over dinner, Lainie relaxed and regaled him with stories of growing up in town. Stories of dances at the city park, floating down either branch of the Platte River in the summer, and skating in the winter. After dinner, they strolled down the street, and she showed him the canteen. They watched as soldiers rushed to reboard a waiting train.

"Come on. Maybe Audrey's here." Lainie pulled him into a large room in the brick building. Tables groaned under the weight of cakes and sandwiches. A coffee urn stood on a table, surrounded by miniature bottles of milk. Other tables were loaded with books and magazines, even a few Bibles. "Every troop train is met by volunteers. We've earned a reputation among servicemen. The best twenty minutes they'll have crossing the country."

"It's impressive."

"You should see us get the men through." Lainie pulled him toward a back room as she talked.

"Hey, Lainie. You back to help tonight?" A nicely plump, older woman waved at them.

"Not tonight. Is Audrey here?"

"No. Should be back tomorrow, though."

"All right. Thanks, Mrs. Edwards." Lainie scanned the kitchen then drew back. "I guess she's not here. We'll catch up with her later. She and her husband live on a ranch north of town. She used to be here all the time." Her expression fell, and she stood as if not sure where to go next. "Guess we might as well look for a movie or something."

"Why don't we grab one of those cherry Cokes you talk so much about? Then we can head back to your house." Tom grabbed her hand and rubbed it. "It can't be as bad as you think it will be."

She searched his eyes, intensity turning hers brown. "You have no idea what my father is like."

"But I'd like to learn. And I can't do that while we hide here."

Lainie harrumphed then shrugged. "Let's get that Coke."

When they returned to Lainie's home, Mason had curled in front of the fireplace, almost as if she'd never left. Lainie's sister sat on the floor, stroking the dog's glossy fur.

"Glad you could bring her home, Lainie. This house has felt like a museum while she was gone."

"It was nice." Mr. Gardner's deep voice echoed in the silence.

"No, I'm glad she's back, too." Mrs. Gardner patted his arm. "You're outnumbered. And I'd suggest you not try something like that again. Mason is part of this family."

He put on a fake pout, though Tom thought he detected a twinkle in the man's eyes. "A man knows when he's beat. Welcome home, Mason."

Mason pricked her ears up—probably at her name—then settled back on the hearth.

৵

Two mornings later, Tom's stomach clenched tightly as he sat with Mr. Gardner. The man had insisted they have lunch together before he and Lainie left. Mr. Gardner leaned back and eyed Tom. "Son, I can tell you care for my daughter."

"Yes, sir. Very much."

"That's all well and good, but she should never marry a soldier."

Tom sagged back in his chair as if punched. "What do you mean?"

"Her mother and I did not raise her to become a widow at a young age. She's also used to the best we could offer.

There's no way you could do that on military wages." He crossed his arms and jutted his chin out even farther.

"That may be so. But I'm unlikely to go overseas, and the war won't continue forever."

"And what are your prospects after that? Have a job lined up as a lawyer or doctor?"

Tom swallowed. He had no real answer, not one that would satisfy this man. "I think I understand."

"I certainly hope so. Nothing against you, but I only want the best for my daughter."

Tom heard the unspoken words loud and clear: *And that's not you.*

twenty-four

July 19, 1943

The ride back to Fort Robinson dragged on, and Lainie could hardly enjoy the scenery or the fact that Mason was safe. After talking to her dad, Tom had crawled into a shell and refused to come out. She could only imagine what Daddy had said. He always knew best. Suddenly Lainie realized that she didn't want him to chase Tom away. Instead, she wanted Tom welcomed with open arms. Based on the set to Tom's jaw and the distant look in his eye, that hadn't happened.

"Look, Tom. I'm sorry about whatever my dad said. He doesn't speak for me."

Tom stared down the road. "I won't go against his wishes."

"But what about mine? Don't I count in this? Aren't I worth fighting for?" Her voice rose with each sentence.

He shook his head. "I can't, Lainie."

She shrank against the seat and turned away from Tom. She was worth fighting for. She was. And if he wouldn't, well, Lainie didn't want to imagine that.

❧

Tom dropped Lainie off and drove to the fort. He parked his car by the barracks but headed for the kennels. When was the last time he had sought out dogs? He couldn't remember.

He walked the perimeter inside the fence. Thoughts raced through his mind. Mr. Gardner's saying his daughter shouldn't marry a soldier colliding with Lainie's insisting she was worth the fight. Yes, she was, but maybe he wasn't the one to do it.

The week passed in a war of emotions. Occasionally he saw Lainie across the yard, but he tried to keep a distance.

He sent others to the K-9 office on errands. The sight of her sent him into a maelstrom of torn emotions. Fight or let her go? Which was best for her? *God, You have to help me.*

Tom took to taking Tornado out most nights for rides. They'd go wherever Tornado wanted to explore. Tom held on and waited for the peace he normally absorbed in the wide-open spaces to find him.

He often took his Bible. When Tornado decided he needed a drink, Tom would hop off and pull his Bible out of a saddlebag. He'd munch on an apple and search the scriptures for something, anything, that felt like direction. The rest of his life was too important to casually throw away. Marriage was also too important to enter knowing that his future father-in-law would never accept him.

Thursday night, Tom followed his new routine. After saddling Tornado, he pointed the horse toward the prisoner-of-war camp. They passed through the empty camp at a canter and soon hit the plains beyond.

After twenty minutes' racing the wind, Tornado stopped beside a stream. Tom ground-hobbled him and grabbed his Bible and snack. He settled on a rock and bit into the apple. Wiping juice from his chin, he turned to the book. Today's devotional reading was Isaiah 43. "When you pass through the waters, I will be with you; and when you pass through the rivers, they will not sweep over you. When you walk through the fire, you will not be burned; the flames will not set you ablaze."

He gazed across the land. Buttes pushed against the sky along the horizon. Last week on the drive to North Platte, he'd passed Lake McConaughy and the Kingsley Dam for the first time. After seeing that body of water, he had a new perspective on what God promised. He would go with him through waters as vast as that lake. If the dam ever gave, water could spill out and overwhelm the north fork of the Platte. The river would lose its lazy quality as water rushed down and overflowed its banks. Even there, God would be with him. If he received orders shipping him overseas and had to walk through the fire of combat, even there God would go with him.

Surely He would see him through this relationship with Lainie. *Lord, give me wisdom. I want to honor You in all I do. But I need Your help to do that here.*

Tom looked back at the Bible. "Do not be afraid, for I am with you. . . ."

That was pretty clear. Time to abandon his fear and walk into the future with God as his guide. In all things. In all situations.

Tornado clomped up to him and pushed Tom's shoulder. He snorted and bumped Tom.

"All right, boy. Let's head back. I've got what I need now." Tom smiled. He did indeed.

⁂

Lainie sat in the rocker on Esther's front porch. August had arrived with a flood of heat and nary a breeze to ease it. She leaned back and let the rocker roll forward, her thoughts wandering.

Tom had disappeared since the trip to North Platte. She'd seen him occasionally but never close enough to even say hello. She'd spent the time working and praying. She didn't want a relationship that wasn't part of God's will for her. Yet Tom set a standard no one else could match.

It had been only three months since she'd arrived in Crawford, but it felt like home. She'd gotten used to seeing people crammed into tiny apartments in little buildings and garages squeezed behind houses. The people had welcomed her, and she couldn't imagine going anywhere else.

But she also couldn't stay if things didn't work out with Tom. It was simply too hard to see him, knowing that their friendship had changed. And just when she'd hoped it would become so much more.

"I think I love you."

Those words continued to echo through her heart, even

as her head argued that he should have emphasized his uncertainty.

The screen door slammed, and Lainie jerked up.

"Lainie, telephone." Tanya grinned at her. "Sounds like a cute one."

Lainie rolled her eyes. No one called her here, so it was likely her boss. She stood and went into the parlor to take the call.

"Hey, Lainie. This is Tom."

Lainie's heart jumped into her throat. She tried to speak but couldn't around the lump.

"Is it. . .is it all right if I come over for a bit tonight? I've missed you."

"It's been hard to tell." She bit her tongue. Why had she said that? "I'm sorry. I'll still be up for an hour if you'd like to come. I think Esther has some pie left from supper."

"I'll be there in ten minutes."

Lainie raced up the stairs to freshen up. She brushed powder on her nose and laughed at the fresh sparkle in her eyes. Didn't take much to resurrect her joy.

She waited in the rocker when he rolled to a stop. As Tom climbed out of the Chevy, she paused, unsure what to expect from him.

"Hey." Tom hesitated at the bottom of the steps then squared his shoulders. He jumped up the steps and sat at her feet. "Lainie, forgive me for being afraid."

"Afraid?"

"Of your father. Of your expectations. Of the future and knowing I can't guarantee what will happen." He grabbed her hands. "Please, Lainie. I'd like another shot."

"What happens the next time you're challenged?"

He pulled back and searched Lainie's face. Heat climbed her cheeks, but she barely breathed as she waited for his reply. He rubbed his thumb over her fingers. Tingles shot up her arm, straight to her heart. If he didn't say something soon, she'd beg him to ignore her remark.

Slowly he nodded as he caressed her hand. "Lainie, I can't promise how I'll react in the future. I can only guarantee you are the most important person in the world to me. I want to give us a chance to build on that. Then we'll see what the future holds."

She nodded. "I really want to see what the future holds for us. Regardless of what Father said, Tom, you are a wonderful man and very special to me."

Lainie hesitated, considering saying she loved him. The rush of emotion she felt every time she thought of him or spent time with him had to be that. But she couldn't say the words, not until he told her he loved her, not just "thought" he loved her.

Tom stood and pulled her to her feet. He caressed her cheek, searching her eyes. She caught her breath.

Was he going to?

She closed her eyes and tipped back her head. In a moment that seemed to last for eternity, she waited. Then he leaned down and kissed her. She eased into the kiss, but he pulled back.

"I think we'd better get inside and grab a piece of that pie."

Lainie opened her eyes and smiled. "That would be safer than kissing in front of all Crawford."

But as they shared a slice of apple pie, Lainie thought she wouldn't mind the extra attention if it meant he'd hold her again.

twenty-five

The sun lit up a cloudless sky on Wednesday, and Lainie rushed through lunch, her plans to ride urging speed. She had the afternoon off and couldn't wait to meet Private Thorson and Daisy at the barn.

Tom waited beside the private, and Lainie rushed up to him for a kiss on the cheek.

"Let me come with you."

"No, this is something I need to do. But you can come find me if I'm gone more than a couple hours. The day is beautiful. Nothing's going to happen."

"Then let me join you."

Lainie shook her head. "I'll be fine." She stepped into the stirrup and threw her leg over Daisy's back. "Meet you at the pool in a couple hours. I'll be there, Tom."

He stepped back but stuffed his hands in his pockets and hunched his shoulders.

Lainie squeezed Daisy with her knees and blew Tom a kiss. "See you soon."

Daisy trotted away from the buildings, and Lainie pulled off her hat and let her hair blow freely in the wind. The trot jolted her too much, so she pulled Daisy to a walk. That didn't stop joy from bubbling through her as Daisy carried her over the plains and picked a path up a butte. When they reached the top, Lainie stopped Daisy and slipped down, the reins clutched in her hand.

She led the horse toward the edge of the butte. Her breath caught at the expanse spread beneath her feet. Off to her right stood a ridge of hills that looked as if God had taken a piece of paper, crumpled it, and then formed the hills to match. Sandwort and miner's candle grew in clumps around her feet, their white flowers brightening the dry landscape.

Lainie walked Daisy along the rim of the butte. She stilled at a clump of creamy yellow flowers she'd never seen before. They looked like tiny fringed orchids with two stripes of red down the middle of each flower, but the flowers stacked like snapdragons. She crouched to examine them and brushed one with her finger. The delicate fringe tickled. She leaned in but couldn't catch a fragrance.

She leaned back on her heels and smiled when Daisy nuzzled her hair. "Wait a moment, girl. We'll leave soon."

She sat and soaked in the sun. It felt like a kiss from heaven. All was right in the world at the moment. Sitting in the middle of God's vast and detailed creation, nothing felt like an insurmountable problem. No, as she examined the fringed flowers, it was clear He cared deeply about everything He made, even a flower no one but Him would see and enjoy.

Closing her eyes, Lainie raised her face. *I will believe that You walk ahead of me into the storms. Thank You for carrying me through this year.*

She inhaled the peace that saturated the air around her. A soft smile touched her face, and she stood. "Let's get back to that wonderful man who loves me."

❧

That week, the girls buzzed with rumors about the new airstrip along the Glen feed area. The army had built the hard-packed dirt strip in one week, but its purpose remained a mystery.

"Maybe they'll bring the POWs in by plane." Mary stood by an open file cabinet.

Kitty shook her head then examined a fingernail she'd been filing. "No. I heard they'll come by train like everyone else."

"Then why build it? It's not like we're the next air base."

Lainie focused on the letter in front of her as the girls continued to chatter. Since it had arrived yesterday, she'd dreaded opening it. The handwriting bore all the marks of her father's, but no return address appeared in the left-hand corner. If it truly was from Father, she didn't know that she wanted to read it. Likely more words about how Tom wasn't the man for her. If only he'd give them a chance to show him the foundation of their relationship.

Some might call it luck or stars aligning in the right configuration, but Lainie knew the fact that she and Tom had even met bore all the hallmarks of the hand of God. Only He could have orchestrated every step of their friendship.

But how to make Daddy understand? The more she worried about it, the more she knew it was out of her hands.

"Lainie." Mary perched on the edge of Lainie's desk. "Are you going to read that or join us in our wild guesses about what's going on?"

Lainie tucked the letter in her desk and shrugged. "Personally, I think they built it as a landing strip for the Germans."

Groans filled the air, and someone pitched wadded-up paper at her. Lainie ducked and laughed with the others.

❧

Tom watched transport trucks roll onto base on August 5. He and the cadre had orders to get the arriving men anything they needed. Only problem was, they still didn't know why the men were here. This operation was cloaked in secrecy so thick no one had penetrated it.

Friday night as he and Lainie walked to a movie, Tom tucked her under his arm and listened as she told him about the speculation in the office. "No one's telling us what's happening. There must be some kind of maneuver."

"But why here?" Lainie leaned into his shoulder. "Fort Robinson isn't easy to find."

"I have a feeling we'll learn more only when we need to know."

Lainie snorted, the unladylike sound making him grin. "That's why you're in the army, and I'm not. I have to know the why. Now."

Tuesday afternoon, the roar of airplanes filled the base. Tom rushed out of the classroom to watch. C-47 transport planes filled the sky, with wingspans of close to one hundred feet. Usually used to carry men and equipment, the behemoths flew east along Soldiers Creek out of the Wood Reserve, pulling smaller planes behind them.

"I ain't seen anything like this before." Sid shielded his eyes.

Tom followed a plane across the sky.

"What are the planes towing?"

John Tyler joined them. "Gliders."

The next day, the instructors were called into a meeting. Tom had heard the gliders were crashing all over the hayfields around the reserve. Sarge Lewis stood at the front of the room, bouncing on his heels.

"War training exercises are happening, and you get to participate. The observing officers want the dogs involved." He rubbed his hands together and grinned. "This is a chance to demonstrate what our dogs can do. Pick two of your teams. You'll go into the field and search for lost and injured soldiers. When you're dismissed, you'll receive maps with your search zones. Good luck, and do us proud."

Tom knew exactly which teams to take. As his mind raced with plans, he rushed out of the room.

"Slow down, Hamilton."

Tom frowned at Sid. "Why? We've got a ton to do to get ready."

"Let's see which team can find the most stranded airmen." Sid slugged him in the arm.

"Deal." Tom couldn't hide his excitement. This is what all the training was about. The teams could demonstrate the value the dogs added to the war effort.

Before first light Wednesday, Tom gathered with his teams and the others to be transported to the drop zone. C-47s continued to ply the sky, and parachutes dotted the sky behind the planes like miniature clouds.

The dogs sniffed the air eagerly, tails standing at attention.

While in the truck, Tom reviewed their assigned sector with his men. "Other teams will serve as sentries, but we're scouts. We'll give the dogs their heads. See what they find. We'll walk the perimeter and then walk in parallel lines until we cover it in a grid."

Privates Jensen and Mueller nodded, their eyes sweeping the map. As soon as the truck stopped, they bounded out with their dogs. Tom watched them start out and followed at a distance. The men and dogs worked as a coordinated team.

Hours later, the sun pounded on Tom. As sweat dripped down his back, he began to envy the remount guys left on base. Both dogs stopped and alerted. Tom scanned the horizon. "See anything?"

Jensen shook his head.

"Over there." Mueller walked with his dog toward a stand of trees. The dog raced the last few feet to the tree and started jumping up its trunk while barking. "We've got a live one."

A colonel, by the eagle on his uniform, hung in a parachute from the branches of a ponderosa pine. As the dog leapt, the officer kicked his legs up. "Get that thing away from me."

Tom stepped forward. "Just a minute, sir. Mueller, pull back with your dog. Be sure to reward him for his good work. Get them ready to continue the search." He put his knife between his teeth and climbed up the tree until he reached the colonel. "I'll cut you down."

"Wait until those dogs are down. What makes them so aggressive?"

"A little horsemeat." At the colonel's twisted face, Tom sawed faster. "Grab hold of the tree, sir."

The man slipped to the ground as soon as he was free of the tangled parachute. The dogs jumped at him, and he leapt backward.

"Sit." The dogs immediately relaxed and obeyed.

The colonel nodded his thanks. "Point me to the nearest command center."

Tom pulled his cap off and scratched his head. Slapping it back on, he shrugged. "I'd tell you if I knew, sir. I'd hike that way if I were you."

The colonel took off, muttering under his breath.

"All right, men. Let's see if we can't find another stranded colonel."

twenty-six

August 11, 1943

Lainie strolled across the highway to the main section of Robinson, keeping one eye on the sky.

"Miss Gardner, a word with you?"

She stopped and found herself face-to-face with Colonel Carr. "Yes, sir."

"It's my understanding you're trained as a nurse."

"Yes, though I haven't used those skills for a while."

"I've heard they're hard to forget. Tomorrow we'll need your services with the maneuvers. The hospital is already engaged with the airmen injured when their gliders crashed."

"Yes, sir." Lainie wanted to tell him that she hadn't enlisted, so she couldn't be commandeered to nurse. But the glint in his eye said that he expected his orders to be followed. She watched him walk to his Jeep and determined to stay on her side of the highway as much as possible. It was far safer.

The next morning, she rose after a restless night. She searched for any argument that she couldn't nurse. The doctors in Kentucky had told her she'd never be able to do that. Her last attempt had ended in disaster when she couldn't keep up with the demands of the doctors. An orderly had physically removed her from the room as her roommate, Roxie, rushed in to fill her place. Her chest tightened and her fingers went numb at the thought of serving as a nurse.

No matter how she searched, there was no way around it. She might be a civilian, but she'd received orders. Lainie slipped beside her bed and prayed for strength to make it through the day. She got up and pulled on a pair of trim denim slacks, a button-front shirt, and saddle shoes, wishing she'd brought her nurse's outfit to Crawford.

Concern edged Esther's expression as she handed a bag breakfast and lunch to Lainie. "Take it easy. You're still recovering from this last bout."

"Esther, you know I love you. It's been a month. I'll be careful, I promise. But I really am doing better."

Esther harrumphed, a touch of worry clouding her expression. "I suppose you're right. Don't overdo."

"I'll probably sit on a chair the whole time." Lainie inhaled the aroma of lemon–poppy seed muffins. "Thanks for this. I have to run before the colonel sends someone after me."

Lainie kept an eye on the sky as she dashed to the shuttle pick-up. Large planes and parachutes filled the sky. Would many men be hurt when landing? She eyed the road, tapping her toes as she waited for the bus. She couldn't do any good waiting here.

Once she reached Fort Robinson, she climbed into a waiting Jeep and was zipped to a staging area. She thanked the soldier for the ride and hopped to the ground. Soldiers hurried in all directions, purpose filling their strides, but none looked familiar. Their patches indicated they weren't from Robinson. Scanning the scene, Lainie headed toward a tent with a painted white circle and red cross.

She pushed the flap aside and stepped inside, giving her eyes a moment to adjust to the dim interior. A nurse slowed down.

"I'm Lainie Gardner. Colonel Carr ordered me to report here."

The woman relaxed and nodded. "We're expecting you, but you're supposed to be a nurse."

"I'm trained as one."

"I'm Nola Grable. Over there are supplies to organize before the rush of today's injuries."

Lainie did as instructed, delighted to work with familiar instruments. "Were there many yesterday?"

"I don't think many of those boys had flown a glider before.

Most crashed. And who would think a hayfield is a good place to hold maneuvers?"

"Only the army?"

Nola laughed and shook her head. "You guessed it. Let's just say I hope these jumpers have more experience."

The first couple of hours were uneventful, so Lainie stayed in the background. A doctor sat while two nurses readied twelve cots in two orderly rows along the back. Nola restocked the pharmaceutical supplies and then joined the doctor. Occasionally soldiers hobbled into the tent, mainly with sprained ankles or twisted knees. Then two soldiers were carted in on stretchers. One had impaled his leg on a small tree, and the other had landed on some rocks and had possible internal injuries.

The doctor barked orders at the nurses. One calmed the man with the tree lodged in his thigh, while the other three worked furiously on the other man.

Lainie moved to the front of the tent, praying God would guide the doctor's hands. Pounding feet rushed toward the tent, and she braced for whatever caused the race. Lainie jumped back when Tom rushed in.

"Lainie, we need the doctor quick." He looked around the tent almost frantically.

"He's working right over there on someone else. What is it? Are you okay?" She reached for his arm, but he brushed past her. A sting of pain pierced Lainie at his snub.

"It's John Tyler. He was attacked by one of the dogs who got too aggressive with a treed parachutist."

"Where is he?"

Tom pivoted and stumbled outdoors. Lainie rushed to catch up with him.

"Are you hurt?" He ignored her and hobbled toward a group of men. "Tom, look at me. What is wrong?" She pulled on his arm until he stopped and looked at her. She frantically inspected him but could not see blood. "Tom!"

"I twisted my leg when I pulled John away from the dog."

He set his chin and looked away. "We're wasting time. John's that way."

Lainie waited a moment then rushed ahead. Tom would relax only when John had the attention he needed. When she reached the cluster of men, she knelt beside John. He lay on his back, blood soaking the front of his shirt and covering his neck.

"What happened?"

Sid started to speak then cleared his throat. "He got between an attacking dog and a soldier. The dog didn't stop and went for his throat. Tom separated them, but he'd already been bit."

Lainie felt a thready pulse on his neck. "Grab that stretcher over there. We'll get him on it and move him to the tent." She jumped up, not waiting to see whether they followed. She grabbed the blankets off a cot and pulled a table of supplies toward it. "Put the stretcher there."

She immediately bent over John's still form. "Stay with me, John." She grabbed bandages and started cleaning the blood so she could see the injuries.

"What have you got, Miss Gardner?" the doctor called from where he worked on the other patient.

"A war dog instructor mauled by a dog. Looks like he was bit primarily on the neck near the jugular."

The doctor whistled. "I'm stuck here, but I'll talk you through it. Have that man beside you apply pressure to the wound."

Lainie looked up to find Tom next to her. He leaned downward to compress John's wound.

"You didn't think I'd leave him."

"What next, Doctor?"

"Is the vein intact?"

Lainie ran her hands through a basin of water and doused them in alcohol. "Lift up for a second, Tom." As soon as he did, she probed the wounds. "I think it's intact."

"You think or you know?"

Lainie closed her eyes and focused on what she could feel. "I'm certain."

"Okay, apply more pressure and clean the wound. When you're sure it's clean, call. One of us will suture him."

John moaned and began to thrash.

"Can I sedate him?"

"Give him a shot of morphine, and get him closed up."

Lainie tried to still her trembling hands as she gave John a shot of morphine. She cleansed the wound and called the doctor.

He looked up. "I can't leave this man. You'll have to suture him."

Lainie nodded and took a deep breath. She threaded the needle. Her stomach clenched as she knelt beside John and the cot. "I'll be gentle." She nodded at Tom. "Lift off unless I ask you to add more pressure."

The metallic smell of the blood overwhelmed Lainie as she worked to stitch the wound together. John and Naomi deserved the best she could give. She tied off the last stitch and leaned back on her heels. She rolled the tension from her neck.

"How's he doing?"

Lainie jumped at Nola's voice. "Okay, I think."

"Good thing you were here. Looks like he's stabilized. Good work." She patted Lainie on the shoulder. "We'll take over."

Lainie looked up and found Tom staring at her, a strange look in his eyes. She tried to stand but felt drained. Tom struggled to his feet and helped her get up.

"Let's get a breath of air."

Lainie gladly accepted his arm and followed him outside. Shivering, she tipped her face toward the sun and soaked in its warmth. The tremors slowly stopped. "Nothing I did in Kentucky felt like that."

"You saved John's life." Tom turned her toward him and pulled her into his arms. "Thank you."

"You saved him first by getting the dog off him. And he's lucky. Since it wasn't his artery, he would have been okay without me." Lainie decided she wanted to spend the rest of the day like this. Wrapped inside the shelter of Tom's embrace. Far from the stuffy hospital tent and the scent of blood. "Are you over your fear?"

Tom nodded, his chin tapping the top of her head. "I think I have been for a while but hadn't stopped to think about it. My accident was a long time ago, and John needed me today. Mason helped, too."

"She is a good dog." Lainie leaned into Tom's embrace for another moment then pushed back. "Time to get back inside. And we need to check out your knee."

Tom grimaced at her.

She laughed and pulled him toward the tent. Her heart sang with the realization her training hadn't been wasted after all. If she'd shipped to Europe as planned, she wouldn't be here right now. And she couldn't think of anywhere else she'd rather be. Or anyone else she wanted to be with.

twenty-seven

September 9, 1943

Tom stepped off the train in Alliance. The town sat sixty miles southeast of the fort and offered more shops than downtown Crawford. He'd been sent to Alliance to accompany another shipment of dogs from Dogs for Defense. He'd arrived early because he had a bit of shopping to do, the kind he couldn't do in Crawford, where word would travel.

Things had quieted down after the glider wars, and he'd spent every free moment with Lainie. That time had only solidified the knowledge in his heart that she was the one. The only one he could imagine spending the rest of his life with.

Oh, she still had the ability to drive him crazy with her sharp tongue. But he'd also seen how deeply she cared about others. The tenacity and stubbornness that drove her when others gave up.

He glanced at his watch. One hour until the train arrived. He'd have to hurry but should have enough time.

※

The office hummed with the usual backdrop of clicking heels, soft voices, and closing file drawers. Lainie leaned away from the typewriter and rolled her neck. The day was almost over. She needed to correct the last mistake and finish the form. She grabbed an eraser from the middle desk drawer.

Lainie heard a crumpling sound as she tried to close the drawer. She frowned and pulled it out again. Slipping her hand inside, she reached back, feeling for whatever might be caught. She groped until she thought her arm would fall asleep but finally felt a piece of paper. Pulling it out, she sat back with a sigh.

She eyed the envelope. It was the one she had received from her dad a month or more ago but never read. She slid a paper opener beneath the flap. The letter was the first and only communication she'd received from her dad since moving to Crawford.

Well, the only way to know what it said was to read it. Pulling out the single sheet, Lainie unfolded it.

Dear Lainie,
 It was a surprise to see you last week with your soldier. Your mother tells me I was too short with him and you. I'd like to blame it on the shock. I only want the best for you. That has been my desire from the moment I first saw you.
 Your mother and I trust you, and we trust your judgment. If you believe this man is the one you want to marry, we will not oppose that. Instead, we both feel peace about it. It helps that his superiors speak highly of him.
 Come home soon. Mason misses you.

Your father

Lainie reread the message, wondering if her eyes deceived her. Did she imagine he'd penned the words? No, he actually was giving his blessing, though in a way that only he would give.

As she read the words, Lainie felt her heart lift. Now there was no reason she and Tom couldn't be together. Closing her eyes, she imagined the next time she would see him. This time without any concerns about what her parents thought about Tom.

Her heart began to pound, and she wished Tom wasn't out of town transporting dogs.

❢

Saturday afternoon, Tom glanced at Lainie. He'd never seen her more beautiful than she looked now, hair bouncing as she cantered over the hills on Daisy. Tornado had no trouble keeping up, and Tom settled back to enjoy the ride.

Lainie had welcomed him with an openness that pleased him. She'd sparred with him on the drive to the stables, yet it held a fun tone that delighted him. There was no question. No one else caused this kind of certainty or knowing in him. He patted the saddlebags to assure himself that he had everything.

Daisy slowed, and Lainie slipped from the saddle. Tom pulled Tornado to a stop.

"Everything okay?"

"Walk with me?" Lainie looked up at him, an impish grin teasing him.

He jumped to the ground, and she reached for his hand. He loved the feel of her small hand tucked inside his. Their fingers twined together, and they ambled toward a butte, the horses trailing behind them. The silence between them was comfortable.

Tornado bumped his shoulder with a snort.

"Cool it, horse."

Lainie laughed. "Are you always so short with Tornado?"

"Only when he forgets his manners."

"He only wants a treat, you know."

"And rudeness is the way to get it." Tom shook his head. "Stand still, Tornado." He unfastened the latch on a saddlebag and reached for the apples he'd tucked inside it. Pulling them out, he also grabbed the present and tucked it into his back pocket, hoping Lainie hadn't noticed.

"What did you just hide?"

So much for that hope.

"Nothing."

"Hmm. Nothing doesn't have to be denied. Come on, show me." She cajoled and tried to reach around him.

Tom danced away and held the apples out. "Don't you want to give one to Daisy?"

"Only after I know what you're hiding from me." She crossed her arms and stuck out her lower lip.

Tom rolled his eyes. "Fine, I'll give Daisy her treat." He

slipped Tornado his apple then turned toward the smaller animal. "Come here, girl. I've got a juicy apple for you."

Daisy tossed her head and snorted.

"See, she wants to know what you're hiding, too."

"Fine. I can't fight two stubborn women."

Lainie laughed and tried to slip around him.

"Hold it right there. Here. Sit on this rock, and close your eyes."

Lainie scrunched her nose and squinted at him.

"I'm serious. Close your eyes."

She shrugged and plopped onto the rock. "Fine."

Tom waved his hand in front of her face, looking for any indication that she was peeking. His stomach fluttered like when he'd eaten too many slices of pie, and he took a deep breath to try to calm it. Couldn't go losing his lunch on Lainie's shoes, nerves or not.

Pulling the small box from his pocket, he popped its lid and stared at the ring. It was simple. A gold band with a tiny diamond. He hoped she liked it. He sank to one knee and blew out a steadying breath.

Lainie bounced her legs and kept her eyes screwed shut. "Ready yet?"

That was his Lainie. Impatient as ever.

"All right, Lainie. Open your eyes."

When she did, her eyes popped wide before she shut them again. She winked one eye and then the other. "What are you doing?" Her voice shook and her legs tapped even faster.

This wasn't the reaction he'd anticipated.

"Lainie Gardner, I've been captivated by you from that first moment you shouted in my ear. You are an amazing woman, and I love you." He reached up to wipe a tear from her cheek. "I cannot imagine my life without you in it. Would you do me the honor of marrying me?"

She nodded and opened her mouth, but nothing came out. She threw her arms around his neck, and he held her as they fell to the ground. Gently he helped her to a sitting position.

She held out her hand, and he slipped the ring from the box and onto her finger. It fit perfectly, just as she fit perfectly in his life.

ಎ

Lainie held up the ring and watched as the sunlight played with the diamond. She could hardly breathe as she tried to comprehend what Tom had offered her. Had he really asked her to marry him? In her dreams, she'd imagined Tom and forever, but she hadn't expected the ring and the promise now. Especially since he hadn't seen Daddy's letter yet.

She searched Tom's face, desperate to find any indication he wasn't sure. All she saw was the quiet certainty and steadiness that personified him. Peace seemed to fill his smile, as if he knew this was the perfect way to spend their future. Her pulse fluttered, and she pulled her gaze back to the ring.

This was real.

"I have something I want to show you, too, Tom." Lainie pulled the envelope from a pocket. "I got this a month ago, but the unopened envelope got mixed into a pile of papers in a desk drawer. I uncovered it earlier this week while you were gone. Here."

Tom looked from her to the letter, concern twisting his face.

"Read it." Lainie twisted the ring on her finger and smiled. He'd decided she was worth fighting for. Even without knowing her daddy agreed.

Tom pulled the letter from the envelope and read. A slow smile spread across his face.

Lainie threw her arms around Tom's neck and hung on. "Are you sure?" she whispered against his neck.

"Absolutely. There is no question in my mind that God has put us together. Are you already having doubts?"

"Only that this is truly happening. I love you, Tom."

"I love you, too, Lainie."

And he sealed his words with a kiss that left her breathless.

epilogue

Lainie pushed back the curtain and looked out the window. She strummed her fingers against the windowpane. Where was the car? Any minute now, Tanya should whip in front of the boardinghouse with Tom's car to carry Lainie to the chapel on base.

It was hard to believe that tonight she and Tom would become husband and wife. A rush of excitement pulsed through her at the thought.

They'd drive to Ogallala and spend the night near Lake McConaughy before continuing to North Platte the next day. Her parents had accepted their decision to have a quick and small wedding but had insisted on a large reception at the Pawnee Hotel ballroom. That was tomorrow. Today they'd have the simple ceremony.

All the girls but Esther had already left. They'd join Tom's army buddies as witnesses.

Lainie turned from the window and smoothed the front of her gown. The pale blue silk swept below her knees and fell in soft pleats. She'd brought the dress to Crawford, not knowing if she would have any occasion to wear it, and now it was her wedding dress. She twirled in front of the window and smiled.

Her bag already sat by the front door, ready to be thrown into the trunk.

"Tanya's here," Esther yelled up the stairs.

Lainie smiled. Her dreams really were going to come true today. She flew down the stairs and into the car, Esther behind her. "Let's go."

It felt as if they would never reach the chapel. Lainie felt tempted to hop out and run to Fort Robinson. Finally, they arrived, and she slipped inside. Tom stood by the chaplain at the front of the small sanctuary. Tanya joined the girls and soldiers who stood in a semicircle up front. Lainie hurried to join them, unable to take her gaze from Tom and the love flowing from him. The ceremony passed in a daze as she stared into his eyes.

This was really happening. He really wanted to spend the rest of his life with her. Lainie closed her eyes and could almost feel the pleasure of heaven.

"You may kiss the bride."

She could feel Tom lean toward her. "Promise me forever, Lainie."

Lainie opened her eyes and smiled at Tom. "With all my heart, now and forever."

He kissed her, and Lainie knew that a dream—one she hadn't even known she had—came true with the promise of a thousand tomorrows filled with love.

A Letter To Our Readers

Dear Reader:

In order that we might better contribute to your reading enjoyment, we would appreciate your taking a few minutes to respond to the following questions. We welcome your comments and read each form and letter we receive. When completed, please return to the following:

Fiction Editor
Heartsong Presents
PO Box 719
Uhrichsville, Ohio 44683

1. Did you enjoy reading *Sandhill Dreams* by Cara C. Putman?
   ❏ Very much! I would like to see more books by this author!
   ❏ Moderately. I would have enjoyed it more if

   _____

   _____

   _____

2. Are you a member of **Heartsong Presents**? ❏ Yes ❏ No
   If no, where did you purchase this book? _____

   _____

3. How would you rate, on a scale from 1 (poor) to 5 (superior), the cover design? _____

4. On a scale from 1 (poor) to 10 (superior), please rate the following elements.

   _____ Heroine   _____ Plot
   _____ Hero   _____ Inspirational theme
   _____ Setting   _____ Secondary characters

5. These characters were special because? _____

_____

_____

6. How has this book inspired your life? _____

_____

_____

7. What settings would you like to see covered in future
   Heartsong Presents books? _____

_____

_____

8. What are some inspirational themes you would like to see
   treated in future books? _____

_____

_____

9. Would you be interested in reading other **Heartsong
   Presents** titles? ❏ Yes   ❏ No

10. Please check your age range:

   ❏ Under 18   ❏ 18-24
   ❏ 25-34   ❏ 35-45
   ❏ 46-55   ❏ Over 55

Name _____

Occupation _____

Address _____

City, State, Zip _____

HEARTSONG
PRESENTS

If you love Christian romance...

$10.⁹⁹

You'll love Heartsong Presents' inspiring and faith-filled romances by today's very best Christian authors...Wanda E. Brunstetter, Mary Connealy, Susan Page Davis, Cathy Marie Hake, and Joyce Livingston, to mention a few!

When you join Heartsong Presents, you'll enjoy four brand-new, mass market, 176-page books—two contemporary and two historical—that will build you up in your faith when you discover God's role in every relationship you read about!

Imagine...four new romances every four weeks—with men and women like you who long to meet the one God has chosen as the love of their lives...all for the low price of $10.99 postpaid.

Mass Market 176 Pages

To join, simply visit www.heartsong presents.com or complete the coupon below and mail it to the address provided.

✂ -

YES! Sign me up for Hearts♥ng!

NEW MEMBERSHIPS WILL BE SHIPPED IMMEDIATELY!
Send no money now. We'll bill you only $10.99 postpaid with your first shipment of four books. Or for faster action, call 1-740-922-7280.

NAME_____

ADDRESS_____

CITY_____ STATE _____ ZIP _____

MAIL TO: HEARTSONG PRESENTS, P.O. Box 721, Uhrichsville, Ohio 44683
or sign up at **WWW.HEARTSONGPRESENTS.COM**